3   5

DATE DUE

3-28-07	
4/11	
7/31/07	
1/19/08	
3/17	
9/23/14 C	
1-30 2a	

DEMCO, INC. 38-2931

THE ENGLISH WIFE

 This Large Print Book carries the Seal of Approval of N.A.V.H.

THE ENGLISH WIFE

DOREEN ROBERTS

THORNDIKE PRESS

An imprint of Thomson Gale, a part of The Thomson Corporation

THOMSON

GALE

Detroit • New York • San Francisco • New Haven, Conn. • Waterville, Maine • London

THOMSON
GALE

Thorndike Press® Large Print Clean Reads.

The text of this Large Print edition is unabridged.

Other aspects of the book may vary from the original edition.

Set in 16 pt. Plantin.

LIBRARY OF CONGRESS CATALOGING-IN-PUBLICATION DATA

Roberts, Doreen, 1934–
The English wife / by Doreen Roberts. — Large print ed.
p. cm. — (Thorndike Press large print clean reads)
ISBN 0-7862-9174-5 (hardcover : alk. paper)
1. Widows — Fiction. 2. England — Fiction. 3. Large type books. I. Title.
PR9199.3.K44228E54 2006
823'.92—dc22
2006028153

U.S. Hardcover:
ISBN 13: 978-0-7862-9174-8
ISBN 10: 0-7862-9174-5

Published in 2006 by arrangement with Harlequin Books S.A.

Printed in the United States of America on permanent paper
10 9 8 7 6 5 4 3 2 1

FROM THE AUTHOR

Dear Reader,

As a young bride, I left my native England and everything near and dear to me to start life over in the U.S. Thirty years later, at the age of fifty-eight, once more I left behind everything that I loved — family, friends and the neighborhood I'd lived in all those years — to drive to the opposite coast and start over again.

The English Wife is Marjorie's story, not mine, but her pain, her fear and her struggles to find her way in an unfamiliar and confusing world are all echoes of my past. Life throws changes at us, some small, some huge. It isn't easy starting over, but we women are strong. When faced with whatever comes next, we struggle to make the best of it in the hopes that the new door will lead us to a measure of peace and, if we're lucky, a better life.

I was one of the lucky ones. I wish all of

you as much happiness as I found in my new life. If you'd like to know more, visit me at www.doreenrobertshight.com.

Always yours,
Doreen Roberts

To my wise and patient editor, Susan Litman. Thank you for all the great suggestions and advice. Your support and encouragement mean everything to me.

To my talented and generous critique partner, Jennifer Hoffman, for taking time out of your own writing to help me with mine. Thanks for challenging me, and for reminding me that there's always room for learning.

To my likewise talented Web pal, Lauren Nichols, for all the times you've let me whine, and all the nice things you've said to make me feel better.

Finally, and most of all, to my dear husband, Bill, for truly listening, for understanding, for loving me enough to give me all the time and space I need — and above all, for keeping your promise and giving me a whole new world.
I'll love you forever.

CHAPTER 1

It's strange how a single sentence can totally change your life. That's all it took to change mine.

I sat in James Starrett's immaculate office, mistakenly thinking that the worst shock of Brandon's death was behind me. Outside the window, rhododendrons soaked up the sun after a long bout of Seattle rain. I wished I could be out there with them, instead of trapped inside that stuffy room. James's voice was enough to send me to sleep as he droned on about the will.

He sat behind a massive desk that gleamed in the rays of sunlight pouring through the window behind him. When he finally paused in his lengthy commentary and raised his eyebrows at me, it took me a moment or two to realize I might have missed something important. I leaned forward. "What did you say?"

He frowned at me over his rimless glasses.

"I was saying, I'd think about selling your property in England."

I groped through the fog in my head to make sense of his words. They seemed to hang in the air between us, about as clear as if he'd spoken in Japanese.

I'd had trouble making sense of anything the past few weeks. At first I couldn't convince myself that Brandon wasn't coming back. Or maybe I was afraid to accept it. As long as I floated along in my little cushion of denial, I wouldn't feel the pain that I knew was waiting to crush me.

I missed him, of course. I kept expecting him to walk in the house, demanding his double-malt scotch, and grumbling because dinner wasn't ready. The house seemed so lonely and empty without him, yet I wasn't hurting the way I thought a new widow should hurt. I kept waiting for that to happen.

I seemed to live in a vacuum, where no one could reach me, and I had to give myself orders so I wouldn't forget to eat or shower or comb my hair. It was a strange existence. I felt like a character living in a book, waiting for the reader to turn another page.

No wonder I couldn't understand James, even though he'd said it twice. I gave him an apologetic smile. "I'm sorry, could you repeat that?"

I didn't like the uncomfortable expression that crept into his colorless eyes. "I said, you need to think about selling your property in England."

I sat staring at him for the longest time, letting the words sink in. Even then, they still didn't make sense. "Property?" My voice sounded as if I'd swallowed sand. "In *England?*"

"Yes." He cleared his throat. "The cottage in Miles End, Devon. It's on half an acre of land, so it should fetch a good price. It's occupied at the moment . . . ah . . . Eileen Robbins is the name . . . but you should be able to get around that. The woman might even be willing to buy it from you. I can put you in touch with a good agent over there, if you like."

I pulled myself upright on the hard chair and shook my head in a vain effort to focus.

James went on in his dry voice as if he were totally unaware of the havoc he was creating in my muddled mind. "Three bedrooms, living room, kitchen and bathroom. I'm told that's considered quite sufficient in a small fishing village like Miles End."

"Village?" I seemed to be repeating words

without understanding any of them.

James looked at me as if I were stupid. I *felt* stupid. How in the world had Brandon kept property in England a secret from me? *Why* had he kept it a secret from me?

My late husband was an investments consultant and wrapped up in his work most of the time. I guess most people would call our life together comfortable. Maybe mundane. Certainly predictable.

Every Friday he and I ate dinner at one of the excellent restaurants in the city. Once a year we'd drive up to Vancouver or take the ferry to Victoria for a week's vacation. That was about the extent of our social life together.

But then Brandon died, and life as I knew it vanished as completely as an early-morning mist on a hot summer's day. Now, three weeks after my husband had been laid to rest, I listened to James drone on and wondered what in the world I was doing there.

"Marjorie?"

I jumped, aware James had asked me a question that had dissolved in my ears before I'd registered it. "Sorry. I didn't get that."

He gave me a pitying look. "I know this must be hard for you. It was a shock to us all. Fifty-four is far too young. We had no idea Brandon had a heart problem. He seemed so healthy and vital."

I doubt even Brandon knew he had a heart problem. If he had, he hadn't thought it worth mentioning to me. It wasn't until the autopsy they found the clogged arteries. My late husband was one of those people who avoided doctors like a vegan avoids mink.

"Marjorie, how much do you know about your financial situation?"

Apparently not enough. Apparently there was a whole lot I hadn't known. I wondered what else he'd kept from me. I had a sudden urge to run from that dismal office with its leathery odor and that awful sickly cologne James wore. I wanted to breathe fresh air, and feel the sun warm on my head. I didn't want to sit there and answer his probing questions.

"Not much." I looked him in the eye. "Brandon took care of all the finances. He was an expert, you know. He didn't trust anyone with his money except himself."

If James detected a slight bitterness to my tone he didn't let on. "Yes, that's what I thought. Judging by your reaction, I assume he neglected to tell you about the cottage."

Good word, neglected. Covered a lot of

sins. It definitely sounded better than out-and-out lying, though technically, I suppose, Brandon hadn't exactly lied. He'd just gone to incredible pains to keep this enormous secret from me. No wonder he had so many business trips to Europe.

I remembered then, something else James had said. I wanted to know more about this woman living in my husband's cottage. Was this a simple business arrangement, an investment, or was she the reason he'd kept it all a secret?

I fought to control my rising suspicions. *Calm down,* I told myself. There could be a lot of reasons why Brandon hadn't wanted me to know he owned a cottage in a foreign country and that a stranger was living in it.

A female stranger.

I couldn't think of one good reason. Except for the obvious. If there's one thing I can't stand, it's being made to look like a fool. Right then I felt like the biggest fool on the planet. "How long has Brandon owned this cottage?"

James flipped over pages for so long I thought he intended to ignore the question. Then he cleared his throat again. "Your husband bought the cottage shortly after your wedding. Three months later, to be exact."

Three months? Was that how long it had taken before Brandon went looking for a diversion? No, I couldn't believe that. Brandon wasn't the type. Besides, I would have known. *Surely I would have known?*

I sat staring at James for quite some time before I finally managed to ask, "Did he say why he bought it?"

"I imagine for an investment."

There. So it was possible. Okay, maybe I was grasping at straws, but I was drowning in a sea of bewilderment and desperately looking for dry land. "So this woman is renting the cottage? Is that it?"

He seemed to have something wrong with his throat because he kept having to clear it. "Not exactly. I believe she's living there free of rent."

"I see." I pulled in a deep, deep breath and let it out slowly. Seconds ticked by while I fought the waves of anger and disbelief. I'd been married twenty-seven years to a man I thought I knew at least reasonably well. Now it seemed I hadn't known him at all.

"Marjorie, you should understand that your financial situation is somewhat delicate."

It took all my willpower to sound indifferent. "I suppose you're going to tell me I'm bankrupt now."

James seemed offended by that. "Bankrupt? Of course not. Brandon was too good a manager to allow that. There are, however, certain matters which have to be addressed."

"What kind of matters?"

He looked down at the papers in front of him. "Well, for one, I'm sure you know that Brandon has made you sole beneficiary of his will."

Well, that came as no big surprise. Brandon had no family living and, to my everlasting regret, we never had children.

"Sole beneficiary," I murmured. "How considerate of him. You're sure he didn't include Eileen what's-her-name?"

Ignoring that completely, James went on talking in that wooden voice of his, seemingly unaware of my growing need to throw something at him. "He's left all his worldly goods to you, with no exceptions. The life insurance should provide you with enough funds to settle immediate matters. You will be receiving a small pension, enough to pay for necessities, though I should caution you that your income will not be as favorable as the one to which you have become accustomed. Since you have at least another fifteen years or so until retirement age, you will most likely have to make some changes."

I was in no mood to sort through all that lawyer-speak. "I assume what all that means is that I have to sell my home."

I could no longer hide my resentment and James's ears turned pink. "By no means. It's a big house for one person, however, and the upkeep must be quite expensive. You might want to consider selling it, yes. Brandon lost money on the stock market and refinanced a couple of years ago, but there should be enough equity left, around thirty thousand or so, to give you a down payment on something a little smaller."

I closed my eyes for a moment. Up until now I'd managed to deal pretty well with the numbing jolts life had just handed me. I'd survived the past three weeks by going back to work at the health club, and must have handled things okay, judging by the comments from my boss, Val Barnes, and the rest of the staff.

True, I didn't like being alone at night, but after I'd locked myself securely in the house and downed two or three glasses of wine, falling asleep hadn't been that difficult. I'd even begun to think about the future and how I wanted to spend the rest of my life.

Moving out of my home, however, hadn't even occurred to me. Right now it was the only stable thing in my life. Losing that would be losing my fragile hold on security.

"I'm sorry, I know how hard this is for you."

God, I wished he'd stop saying that. How could he possibly know what it felt like to lose everything that had formed the basis of my life for all these years.

"Apart from the mortgage on your house, you have no outstanding debts," James said. "That leaves the property in England. You own that free and clear. The money you get from the sale should help considerably. I understand it's worth around three hundred thousand, though of course, bringing that amount of money into this country will mean taxes. . . ."

The cottage. For a moment I'd almost forgotten about it. I wanted to forget about it. Forget Eileen what's-her-name ever existed. Forget the doubts poisoning my mind.

But I couldn't. I wanted to know if Brandon had been having an affair with this woman all these years. Or maybe she was the latest in a string of affairs. Maybe that was the reason he'd bought the cottage in a remote village in England, so he could conduct his romances in complete assurance that I'd never find out.

If so, then why the hell did he marry me? Why did he stay married to me if he didn't love me?

The questions were driving me crazy. I found it impossible to believe that the meticulous, distant man I'd lived with for so long could have led a double life of deceit and infidelity. I just couldn't imagine him getting passionate over any woman. He certainly never showed much passion toward me.

A thought struck me, and although I hated asking, I really needed to know. "Does this Eileen person know that Brandon died?"

James wore his usual pained expression. "It's not my place to inform Ms. Robbins. As the owner of the cottage, that will be up to you."

I stared at him for a long moment. I couldn't be sure that Brandon had a personal relationship with this woman. I could be jumping to conclusions, condemning my husband without any grounds other than circumstantial evidence.

On the other hand, if it *was* personal, I just couldn't send her a blunt note telling her the man with whom she might be having an affair had died.

Phone call? Perhaps. Even as I considered it, I knew I couldn't do that, either. I couldn't talk to the woman without knowing the answers.

Which led to another burning question. *Did she know about me?*

Suddenly, I'd had enough. I gathered up my purse and scrambled to my feet. "I'm sorry, I have to go. I'm needed at work."

James dropped the papers he'd held, and for the first time a flicker of anxiety crossed his face. "We're not quite finished here, Marjorie. There are papers to sign, a few more concerns to go over, decisions to be made —"

"Not now!"

My sharp tone must have surprised him. He raised his eyebrows again and a red spot appeared in each cheek. He started to get up, but I waved a hand at him.

"I'll call you. I need time to think about everything."

To my horror I felt my control crumbling. I had to get out of there. Now, before I made a complete and utter fool of myself. I fled for the door, dragged it open and didn't bother to close it behind me.

Melanie, James's pinched-face assistant, said something to me as I hurried past her desk, but I couldn't look at her. I just kept going and didn't stop until I reached my car in the crowded parking lot of the office complex.

Tears spilled down my face as I got the door open and scrambled inside. My nice safe cushion had collapsed. Now that I no longer had to put up a brave front, I could give in to the pain that finally racked my body. I rested my arms on the wheel, buried my face in them and opened up the dam.

I was nineteen and incredibly naive when I'd married Brandon. Ten years before that my father had stepped on a mine in Vietnam and my mother never recovered. She shut herself away from the world and her only daughter.

I'd been lonely for too long when Brandon walked into the hotel where I worked as a desk clerk. He was new in town and I suggested a few good restaurants. To my surprise he invited me to join him for dinner, and I ended up helping him find a place to live.

He was eight years older than me, good-looking, confident, sophisticated — all the things I wasn't. He made me feel safe just by being with him. Looking back, I guess he was the protective father figure I'd missed so terribly during my formative years.

There was something else, an air of sadness about him, as if he'd suffered some deep emotional trauma that he was determined to keep to himself, no matter how hard I tried to draw him out.

It was that melancholy that convinced me I should marry him. I thought perhaps we could heal each other. I was wrong. I never could reach that inner part of him, and after a while I gave up trying.

I asked him once why he'd married me. He'd given me that sad smile and murmured, "Because you needed me." I'd had the feeling then that Brandon needed to be needed, and I was the first one to give him that.

But not the last, if my suspicions were correct.

When I reached the health club I did my best to mop up the ravages of my pity party, but I still looked as if I'd contracted some deadly disease. Blotched skin, bloodshot puffy eyes, red nose — crying always does that to me.

Val sat at my desk in the throes of a heated discussion with a customer. The young blonde's vivid orange sweats clashed horribly with the pale pink palm trees decorating the lobby. Usually our clientele had better taste than that.

Their raised voices echoed far enough to turn the heads of some clients on the other side of the glass wall behind Val. I hurried over there, my own problems momentarily forgotten.

Val's relieved expression went a long way toward restoring some of my self-esteem as I explained to the irate customer that her payment had arrived too late to credit her last bill. I promised the matter would be taken care of immediately.

As the young woman stalked off, Val rolled her eyes. "Thank God you got here. You know how useless I am at bookkeeping. The damn woman was getting hostile. I was just about to call security."

"We don't have security." I took the chair she'd just vacated and reached for the morning mail.

"Well, we should get some. It's times like these —" She broke off with a muttered exclamation. "Holy crap, Margie. What happened to you?"

I'd avoided looking directly at her until now. I didn't need a mirror to know why she stared at me as if I'd grown horns. "I'll tell you later," I mumbled.

"You'll tell me now." She looked at the

slim gold watch on her wrist. "Come on, let's go eat."

"But I just got here."

"Yes, and over lunch you can tell me what you've been doing all morning to destroy your face." She grabbed my arm and pulled me up off the chair.

She was used to getting her own way, and since she was my boss I didn't waste time arguing with her. I followed her to the cafeteria, miserably aware that she would not be satisfied until she'd wrung every last detail out of me.

CHAPTER 2

When it had become obvious Brandon and I would not be blessed with children, I'd taken accounting classes at business school and for years I'd worked for my dentist until he retired.

When I saw the ad for a bookkeeper at a new health club, I couldn't resist applying. I did it to show Brandon he wasn't in total control of my life, but after talking to Val, it seemed such a happy place compared to the long faces at the dentist's office, and I was overjoyed when she hired me. Brandon, of course, was horrified.

Over the six years I worked for Val I learned a lot about running a business, and ended up taking over most of the paperwork involved. Val was ten years younger than me and happily divorced, with alimony that would have paid my mortgage twice over. She kept trying to get me physically trained. I absolutely refused. Cramming my body into skintight clothes and bouncing around among all those nubile goddesses was not my idea of a good time. I'd never have a figure like Val's, no matter how much I sweated and starved. I'd accepted that, even if Val wouldn't.

Seated opposite me at a vinyl covered table in the club's cafeteria, she studied my face. "We should be in a bar with a bottle of good Scotch. You look as if you could use one."

The idea was tempting. "I've had a bad morning." The understatement of the century, but I wasn't ready to share my suspicions about my late husband's activities just yet.

All around me young women in tight outfits were battling to be heard above each other's chatter. The babble did nothing to soothe my frayed nerves. The price I paid for a free lunch.

I should have known I couldn't fool Val. She pursed her perfectly outlined lips. "You've been doing so well up to now. Just tell me what happened."

Giving up hope of keeping the news to myself, I explained about the cottage and the mystery woman, though I left out all my suspicions. I guess I was hoping Val would dismiss the whole thing as insignificant.

She'd never been blessed with tact. "Are you telling me Brandon had a mistress? God, I didn't think he had it in him. Just goes to show you can't tell a book —" She slapped a hand over her mouth. "Oh, God, Margie, I'm sorry. This must be tough on you. No wonder you look like crap. It's hard enough to lose a husband, but to find out he's been cheating on you . . ." Her voice trailed off, and tears of sympathy glistened in her gorgeous violet eyes.

I was pretty sure the tears were genuine. Val could be as tough as nails about most things, but if you were a friend in need, she was there for you. To hear her confirm my misgivings almost wrecked the careful hold I had on my composure.

Even so, for some unfathomable reason, I struggled to give Brandon the benefit of the doubt. "I don't know that he cheated on me. There could be a dozen reasons why he let this woman live there rent-free."

"Yeah? Name one."

I groped for possibilities. "She could be a relative, or an important client."

"So why didn't he tell you?"

The hollow feeling I'd been fighting all morning invaded my stomach. I reached for the pepper shaker and sprinkled a liberal amount into my soup. "Okay, so I don't know."

Val's eyes gleamed with anticipation. "Well, there's one way to find out."

"How?"

"By going there and confronting her."

"Go to England? You've got to be kidding."

"Why not? At least you'd find out for sure what Brandon was up to, and England is supposed to be beautiful this time of year. All those yards in full bloom, boating on the lake, garden parties, afternoon teas, flower shows . . ." She clasped her hands and gazed up at the ceiling. "Fabulous. If I had an excuse to get out of Seattle for a while I'd be on the plane tomorrow."

"You watch too much TV." I picked up my spoon and tasted the soup. It needed more pepper. "James told me that Miles End is a little fishing village on the southwest coast. It's probably smelly, grubby and full of sweaty fishermen who haven't looked at a shower in days. I'd have to stay in some smoky, grimy pub where I'd be kept awake half the night by the drunken brawls."

Val grinned. "Obviously we watch different movies. Seriously, though, Margie. Think about it. You actually own a cottage in England. What are you going to do with it?"

I didn't want to think about the cottage. Just the mention of it made me want to dig up Brandon and wring his deceiving neck. My voice was abrupt when I answered her. "Sell it, I guess. Get it out of my life. Forget it ever existed."

"Why don't you just throw her out and rent it."

I had to admit, the idea had merit. Then again, we were both jumping to conclusions. The poor woman could be totally innocent and have a perfectly legitimate reason for enjoying a rent-free existence.

Just to torment me, snippets of items I'd read about well-heeled business men renting luxury penthouse suites for their paramours danced gleefully through my head.

I banished them from my mind. For one thing, if what James said was true, my husband had not been that well-heeled. For another, why go to all that trouble and expense to buy a cottage in England, when surely it would have been cheaper to rent something in the U.S.?

Something just didn't fit, and much as I hated to acknowledge the fact, I was dying to get to the bottom of the mystery. On the other hand, to let Val know that was inviting an exhaustive campaign to send me over there. I definitely wasn't ready for that.

"No," I said firmly. "I just want to get rid of the damn thing." I pushed the soup away from me, picked up the long dessert spoon and jammed it into my mushy frozen yogurt.

Val was not about to give up that easily. Once she got excited about an idea she refused to let go. "Well, then, if you're going to sell it, wouldn't it make sense to go over there to protect your interests? How do you know if you're getting a fair price and that everything is aboveboard if you're not there to keep an eye on the proceedings?"

I sent her a look that I hoped conveyed my loathing for that idea. It was all very well for her to give me advice. After all, she was used to living on the edge. She met guys through the Internet and dated them. That sounded a tad risky to me, but Val's favorite saying was "If you're not risking, you're not living," so I kept my thoughts to myself.

"James gave me the name of a reliable agent." I reached for my diet soda. "I'm sure the man knows what he's doing."

"How can you be sure? You don't even trust that creepy lawyer. How can you trust someone you've never met?" She leaned forward, her face glowing with excitement. "Just think. You could hook up with a good-looking, romantic young Englishman over there."

The idea was so ridiculous I'd have laughed if I hadn't been simmering with all that resentment. "Val, I'm a forty-six-year-old widow. Look at me. Do I look like I'm ready for a romance?"

She studied me for a moment. Her thick blond hair was cut short, like a man's. It looked great on her, but it wouldn't have worked on me. My hair was too baby-fine. I let it hang around my face to hide my wrinkles.

After a moment, Val nodded. "You look great for your age. Besides, someone told me the young Brits love older women. They call it granny grabbing, or something like that."

I choked, almost spitting a mouthful of soda across the table. "How terribly romantic," I said, when I could stop coughing.

"Well, I think it is." She actually looked offended.

I shook my head at her. "Brandon's only been dead a month. I'm still trying to deal with that. The last thing I need is another man. Period."

She sat back, obviously disappointed. "Well, you can't say you had a wildly passionate marriage. In all the times I saw you two together, I never once saw Brandon hold your hand or even touch you."

I pretended to be interested in the fizzy contents of my glass. True, Brandon hadn't been into heavy petting. On the rare occasion he'd felt amorous he'd conducted the whole business with his usual precision, and finished up with his customary peck on the cheek.

I'd reached the stage when it didn't bother me that much anymore. It did bother me, I was surprised to discover, that other people had noticed his lack of affection.

"He wasn't the romantic type," I murmured. "You know that. He had trouble expressing his feelings."

"He didn't have any trouble expressing them in England, apparently." She must have seen me flinch, because she hurried to add just the right tinge of sympathy. "Although I'm sure Brandon loved you. In his own way."

I almost laughed at that. "Who knows what Brandon felt, and who cares."

"You do," Val said softly. "I'm sorry, Margie. I know how much this must hurt."

She was right. It did hurt. On the surface I'd had everything a woman needed to be content. I had a nice home, no worries to speak of, and I had companionship. I could wake up during the night, reassured by the sound of snoring next to me. Even when Brandon left on his business trips, I didn't feel really alone. I knew he was coming back in a few days. I'd had security, the one thing I valued above all else.

Security wasn't something I took for granted. I was still a young child when my mother sank into her depression after my father died. She'd gone back to bartending, and buried herself in her job. I was left to fend for myself.

I didn't bother much with friends. I guess I was ashamed of the pigsty we lived in, and the empty bottles of booze in the sink.

Brandon came into my life shortly after she died. And maybe he wasn't the prince of my dreams, maybe we weren't consumed with passion like the characters in my favorite books, but I believed we loved each other and he offered me the security I'd never had. Or so I'd thought. Considering what I'd just learned, my life hadn't been all that secure after all.

Determined not to let Val's well-meant sympathy drag me down again, I chugged my soda. "I'm not going to waste my time obsessing over something that might never have happened. There has to be a completely valid reason for all this."

"A reason for another woman to be living rent-free in a cottage you knew nothing about?" Val shook her head. "Get real, Marjorie. Stop making excuses for that bum."

Okay, so maybe I was making excuses for him. Maybe I wasn't ready to accept the fact I'd been that dense that I couldn't see what was going on under my nose. I'd thought we were reasonably content with each other.

True, I'd always known something was missing. There were even times, when his arrogance and insensitivity got a little tough to put up with, that I wondered why I stayed with him.

I guess it was that security thing again. I had too many vivid memories of revolting leftovers and freezing nights in our miserable apartment.

How'd that saying go? *Better the devil you know, than the devil you don't.* Well, Brandon Maitland was my devil and until now I'd considered it a fair exchange.

"He practically ran your life," Val said, echoing my thoughts. "Look what good it did you. Here you've got a chance to see another part of the world and you're afraid to take it."

That stung. "Hey, it wasn't that bad. Brandon liked to be in charge, sure, and I was okay with that, as long as I had my job and my own interests. I'm not afraid to go to England. I'm just not that interested."

"That's hogwash. Aren't you just the tiniest bit curious? Don't you even want to know what she looks like?"

"Not at all." I was lying through my teeth, of course. I was eaten up with curiosity.

Val leaned toward me again, her eyes willing me to agree. "Come on, Margie. It's time to start taking risks. You don't have Brandon breathing down your neck anymore. You're free, girl! Go for it! Go to England, tell that tramp what you think of her and throw her out of your cottage. Then go have yourself one hell of a vacation."

The waiter arrived with the bill just then, saving me from answering right away. This was a mistake, I thought. I should have gone home instead of going back to work. I needed time to absorb all this.

I wanted a hot bath, perfumed oil, candles, a bottle of wine and a good book. I wanted to throw my clothes all over the bedroom, leave dirty dishes in the sink, turn the CD player on full blast, now that Brandon wasn't there to frown his disapproval.

I didn't want to think about the cottage, or what it might mean. Not now. Not yet. Right now I wanted to be alone, to pamper myself, and give myself time to recover.

I'd spent twenty-seven years with a man who'd been leading a secret life. All those years I'd put up with his overbearing attitude and his annoying little habits, telling myself I was better off with him than without him. How wrong could I have been.

Well, now he was gone, and he couldn't hold me back anymore. I still missed him, more than he deserved, but now I wanted to be done mourning and get on with my life. The sooner the better.

I soon found it wasn't that easy to get back to normal. Val insisted I go home after lunch, and I was only too happy to agree. I needed to be alone to think.

After all, I was pretty much used to doing things on my own. I didn't make friends easily — a throwback, no doubt, to my lonely upbringing. Once you get used to doing without people, it becomes a habit.

With the exception of Val, the few women I knew well enough to call friends were wives of Brandon's business cronies, and had faded out of my life within a few days of the funeral. I didn't miss them.

As for all those young women at the health club — well, they were mostly athletic types with a focus on perfecting their image and an annoying penchant for trying to outdo each other. All that competitiveness was not for me. I just wasn't in their league.

I was comfortable in my own company, but as I sat outside the house I'd shared with Brandon, I felt an odd reluctance to go back in there. The memories mocked me, as if chiding me for being so trusting, so accommodating all these years. I'd taken the easier path, and I had only myself to blame if I'd missed the signals.

I climbed out of the car and left it at the curb. I still couldn't go back into the garage. That's where I'd found Brandon, that awful night I'd arrived home to see him sprawled half in, half out of his BMW, his head on the ground, those cold blue eyes of his wide open and staring at nothing.

He'd managed to stop the car, though it was angled across the entrance. The heart attack must have hit him before he got to the driveway. Brandon was fussy about parking in the exact same spot every single time. Then again, Brandon was fussy about everything. He wouldn't have appreciated being seen by strangers with his hair all mussed and his butt in the air.

I let myself into the house, conscious of the deathly quiet with the door closed on the outside world. I decided to forgo the wine that evening. I didn't want it to become a crutch.

I woke up in the middle of the night, as I'd done for the past three weeks, expecting to hear Brandon snoring next to me. Listening to the house creak and crack in the dark, I thought again about the woman who lived alone in the cottage.

Was she lying awake, too, wondering why Brandon hadn't been in touch with her? How had he kept in touch with her? The phone? Letters? E-mail? There had to be records of some sort. Or had he ignored her once he was back home, as he'd so often ignored me?

Memories invaded my mind, little things that had meant nothing at the time but now seemed significant in light of what I now knew. The evenings when we'd be watching TV and I'd catch him staring into space, oblivious of what was playing on the screen in front of him. I'd assumed he was thinking about his work, but now I wondered if he was thinking about her.

I tossed over onto my other side and pummeled the pillow. I had to stop all this guesswork. Tomorrow I'd search the room he'd used as an office, and see if I could find any clues to the cottage and its mystery occupant.

I slept through the alarm the next morning. Staring at the neat row of suits, dresses and skirts in my closet, I couldn't decide what to wear. For once, the thought of sitting at that desk, smiling at all those fresh, eager faces with their perfect figures and their perfect lives depressed me.

Not only that, I just couldn't handle the prospect of having to field another barrage of questions from Val. I needed some time off. I had some huge decisions to make, stuff to take care of and I simply wanted to be alone for a while.

I called Val. She was understanding, considering I'd left her stranded without a bookkeeper or receptionist. "Don't worry," she assured me. "I'll get a temp until you feel like coming back."

"I don't know how long —" I started to say, but she interrupted me.

"Take as long as you need. Is there anything I can do? Let me know if you think of something."

I heard agitated voices in the background just before she hung up, and guilt pricked at me for letting her down. I felt better after I'd showered, but I put off going into Brandon's office until I'd drunk two cups of coffee and finished off a box of cereal.

I walked down the passageway to the office and threw open the door. After being shut up for so long the room smelled of worn clothing and rotting apples.

As always, Brandon's desk had been cleared, except for a neat pile of papers sitting in the tray I'd bought him for Christmas one year.

I flipped through them, finding nothing more exciting than a few bills, all of which had been paid after I got the second notices. The telephone bill was tucked in with them, but I could find no records of a call to Devon, England. Of course not. He would have called from work. He wasn't a stupid man.

I turned on the computer and played with several possible combinations of words and numbers, knowing all the time how futile it was. Brandon's e-mail would be lost forever. In any case, he'd have used his work computer if he wanted to hide anything from me.

The lower drawer held a number of files, all neatly labeled. I flipped through them but couldn't see anything connected to a cottage in England. I should have known he was too clever to leave clues lying around for me to find. Obviously he wasn't as trusting as I had been.

I gave up and went back into the living room, where I called James. Melanie answered, and I made an appointment to see him. I still had papers to sign, and I wanted the address and phone number of that darn cottage. I didn't know what I was going to do with it yet, but I'd feel better knowing how to get in touch with *her.*

The days after that stretched before me without any real purpose, and I felt lost, wondering if I'd made a mistake by taking time off. The house seemed so empty and silent.

At first I filled my time by cleaning all the corners that sometimes got neglected during normal housework. I shoved furniture around and rearranged everything, polished windows and washed all the light fixtures.

I sorted out drawers, cupboards and shelves, managing to avoid Brandon's closet, his dresser and his office. I'd exhausted the contents of the kitchen cabinets, and I went grocery shopping, coming home loaded with frozen dinners, packages of cookies and gallons of ice cream.

The television kept my evenings occupied until well into the night. I slept until late the next morning, and lived in jeans and oversize shirts. Val kept calling to ask me to lunch, but I couldn't be bothered to get dressed up, much less face her constant chatter, so I made excuses until finally she stopped calling.

Through it all, an underlying guilt kept nagging at me. Thousands of miles away, a woman waited for a word, a letter, an e-mail or a phone call that would never come. James had given me the address and phone number, but I couldn't seem to make a decision on what to do about it.

The questions still haunted me. Was she suffering, wondering why she'd been abandoned? Or was she innocent of any wrongdoing, going on with her life, happily unaware that her free ride in the cottage was about to end?

Each time I thought about her I pushed the questions to the back of my mind. I'd deal with that problem later, I told myself. When I felt stronger. After all, there was plenty of time. Or so I thought.

CHAPTER 3

Val called the day before the Fourth of July holiday. "Come on over," she said, her voice brittle with forced enthusiasm. "I'm having a barbecue. Just a few friends, you don't have to bring anything. You need to get out of that house. Besides, there's someone I want you to meet."

The thought that she might want me to meet one of her computer dates scared me. I tried to sound appreciative. "Thanks, Val, but I already have plans."

I could tell she was miffed when she answered. "Well, don't say I didn't try. You'll be missing a great party."

"I know. Thanks for thinking of me." I hung up, wondering how she could have known me for six years without realizing I wasn't a party person.

A month after that I sat down one afternoon to pay the bills and realized there wasn't enough left in the bank to pay the mortgage for longer than three months. It was wake-up time. I had to go back to work.

I paced around my spotless house, arguing with myself over my next move. I had to get on with my life, that much was obvious. Decisions had to be made. One thing was certain — I didn't want to go back to the health club.

What I needed was to put the past firmly behind me and start over. I wanted a new place to live, a new job, a whole new life. I'd wasted enough of the former one. I had a lot of catching up to do.

I went back to the kitchen table and studied the bank accounts and the bills I owed. It dawned on me then that I couldn't put the past behind me until I'd dealt with it. I had a house I couldn't afford to live in for much longer, and property in England that wasn't producing one cent of income, yet had to be accumulating debts, like taxes and maintenance. It was time to sell them both.

I wondered where Brandon had kept all the papers on the cottage. His company had sent home his personal belongings from his office, but I still hadn't opened the box. I went to get it from the spare bedroom, where I'd dumped it on the bed.

There wasn't much in it except a few

books, a little stand with his name tag on it, a few CDs of jazz music and a slew of receipts for his expenses, which I assume had been paid with his last salary check. Nothing that had anything to do with property overseas. No photo of me to stand on his desk. Trust Brandon to prefer gazing at his own name rather than a picture of his wife.

Having drawn a blank on that issue, I called Val, and after some hedging around, told her I wanted to quit.

"You're not serious!" she said, sounding more upset than I'd expected. "So are you going to England?"

"No, of course not." I tried to think of a diplomatic way to say it. "I just think I need something a little more rewarding if I'm going to make a career of it. I thought I might do something with children, maybe office work in a school or something."

"Well, you can't quit. You're the best bookkeeper I've ever had. You know just as much about the business as I do. Besides that, you're the only woman I know who isn't into competing with me."

"That's because I'd lose. I'm sorry, Val. I'll really miss you."

"Hey, just because you won't be working for me doesn't mean we can't ever see each other, does it?" Doubt crept into her voice. "Are you sure this is what you want?"

I wasn't sure of anything right then, but I didn't want to admit that. "Quite sure."

"Have you decided what you're going to do with the cottage in England?"

I was expecting the question, but not the sudden stab of resentment. "No, I haven't. I'm sorry, Val. There's someone at the door. I have to go." When did I get so adept at lying, I wondered.

"Let's have lunch," Val said urgently. "Today. You've got to get out of that house."

I muttered something about next week and hung up.

Determined not to fall back into that awful inertia, I took a walk in the park. The August sun had dried out the grass, leaving brown patches despite the sprinklers that must have worked overtime to compensate for the lack of rain. We were in midsummer already, and I'd lost the past two months in a haze of laziness and procrastination.

I sat on a sun-warmed bench and tried to empty my mind, to let the surroundings soak into me. Joggers loped along the curving path between the trees, dodging around the two elderly women engaged in what appeared to be an intriguing and highly amusing conversation. I couldn't help wondering if I'd ever feel like laughing again.

In front of me, two little girls chased each other around the swings. Listening to their squeals, I envied their blissful ignorance of life's brutal punches. How I wished I were a child again, with my whole life ahead of me and choices still to be made.

As I watched, one little girl fell on her knees and started to cry. Out of nowhere an elderly woman rushed toward her and gathered her up in her arms. The tug I felt then had nothing to do with being young and making choices.

If I hadn't married Brandon I might have had grandchildren by now. I'd wasted so many years, and now it was too late. I'd never have a child of my own, never see grandchildren grow up, never know what it was to tuck up a child in bed and read bedtime stories, or watch a daughter walk down the aisle as a beautiful bride. So many wonderful moments I'd missed.

Brandon had told me shortly before we were married that thanks to a vicious bout of mumps in his teens, he was sterile. At the time it hadn't seemed to matter that much. I was young, looking at a secure future, and vague thoughts of adoption had calmed the doubts. But then, as I matured, the mothering instinct had taken over.

Brandon absolutely refused to consider adoption, or any artificial means of having a child. Maybe if he'd given me the affection I'd needed, opened up to me, let me in to that private world he'd guarded so zealously, I could have found comfort in that. As it was I found other compensations — in my job, and eventually in music and in books, just as I had as a child.

Now, thinking about how he'd deceived me, I was boiling with anger and regret for all the things I'd given up for him.

I had to stop wallowing in resentment. It wasn't Brandon's fault he was sterile. He certainly didn't ask to die suddenly and leave me alone. As for the business with the cottage, I had no real reason to suspect him of cheating on me. I had no proof, and I should know better.

I was forty-six years old, and I still had a life to live. I still had time for choices, good or bad. All I had to do was find the strength to make them.

Fueled by my determination to move on, the following morning I tackled Brandon's closet. The faint remnants of his cologne still clung to his suits, and the robe he always wore at night hung above his neatly placed slippers.

I lifted it from its hook and immediately a

voice in my head wondered if he'd worn a robe when he was with *her.* No matter how hard I tried I couldn't seem to get rid of my ridiculous suspicions.

Irritated with myself, I pulled suits, shirts, jackets and pants from their hangers and threw them in an untidy heap on the bed. I piled shoes, ties and underwear on top of them, then found a box of black plastic yard bags. After stuffing them full I hauled them out to the garage. The next local charity drive would reap a bonanza.

Brandon's face came back to haunt me as I walked back into the house. How he would have hated to see his clothes tossed out in such a cavalier way. I felt a stab of guilt, then got annoyed at the thought that he could still reach out from the grave to criticize me.

On impulse I called Val. "How about lunch?" I said, as soon as she answered. "Today?"

"What's happened?" Her voice vibrated with curiosity. "You've decided to go to England?"

Once more I had the feeling of air being snatched out of my lungs. The reminder that I still had a huge problem to deal with threatened to undermine my resolve. "No, of course not. I'm tired of talking to myself, that's all. I need some real conversation with another human being."

"That I can do." She hesitated, and her voice turned wary when she added, "Ah . . . did you change your mind about coming back to work?"

"I'm not asking you for my job back, if that's what you mean." I thought that sounded a bit abrupt and hurried to reassure her. "I've put in an application with the school district, but I haven't heard anything yet."

She sounded relieved when she answered, and I figured she'd already replaced me. We arranged a time and place and I hung up, feeling more positive than I could have imagined two months ago. I was going to make it. I'd survived the worst and I had nowhere to go but up. At last life was beginning to look good again.

I met Val in a quiet little restaurant on the edge of town. With its paneled walls, white tablecloths and soft music playing in the background, it provided a welcome contrast to the health club's noisy cafeteria.

She arrived late, falling onto her chair with a flurry of apologies. "Damn traffic, I swear it's getting worse. I had two calls just as I was leaving. We really miss you at the club,

Margie. Things haven't been the same since you left."

Thinking about those days of striving to please all those demanding women, I knew I'd made the right decision. After we both ordered chicken Caesar salads, I listened while Val told me about her latest adventure with a computer date.

"I was having a good time until he said he'd left his wallet at home. I ended up paying for the meal. Then he asks to borrow cab fare. Hello? I told him he could freaking walk home. Jerk." She snorted in disgust and took a swallow of the chardonnay the waiter had just put down in front of her.

For the first time in weeks I felt like laughing. I bit my lip instead.

"What about you?" she demanded, her eyes narrowing. "You look like you've lost some weight."

Fifteen pounds to be exact, but I didn't want to admit to that. "A little," I said instead. "I'm doing fine. I'm getting used to being on my own. I'm sleeping better and getting things done around the house."

"Way to go," Val murmured. "But what about the cottage? Have you sold it yet? Are you going to England?"

I waited for the hollow feeling to pass before answering untruthfully, "I haven't given it much thought lately. I've had other things on my mind."

"Like what?"

I reached for my own glass of wine. "Well, like getting a job. Selling my house."

Val's jaw dropped. "You're going to sell your *house?* Why?"

"It's too big for one person, too expensive." *Too many memories,* I added mentally.

Her eyes lit up. "All right! Can I go house hunting with you?"

I hadn't thought that far ahead. The idea of buying another house was unnerving. "I was thinking more of renting."

"Even better. We can go look for apartments."

I didn't want to go apartment hunting with Val. She'd force her ideas on me as usual, I'd insist on sticking with mine and she'd get miffed. I changed the subject. "So tell me all about the club. What's been happening since I left?"

Fortunately she was happy to fill me in, and we'd eaten our salads by the time she'd finished. Having exhausted her topic, once more she scrutinized my face. "So what about you? You haven't been moping around the house all this time, have you?"

"I've kept busy." I fiddled with my glass, even though it was empty.

"Margie, don't you have friends, relatives you can visit? You shouldn't be spending all this time alone."

"I don't mind being alone, and I'll be working again soon."

She pursed her lips. "You don't make friends easily, do you? I've known you for six years, and I feel as if I don't really know you at all. Except you weren't happy, and didn't want to talk about it."

I stared at her. "What made you think I was unhappy?"

"Well, weren't you unhappy?"

"I wouldn't say that. Brandon and I had our differences but we rarely argued."

"That's because you were never together. You led separate lives from what I could tell."

I hadn't realized I'd given so much away. "Well, Brandon wasn't much of a talker," I said carefully.

"But what about friends? You must have had girlfriends you could talk to, have a laugh with and hang out together?"

"Not really. I've never been much on girl talk."

Val crossed her arms and I knew I was in for one of her lectures. "Margie, you're a nice person. A good person. But it's time you started living. I mean really living."

I knew what she meant by that. Computer dates, noisy, smoky bars, crowded dance floors. The very thought of it made me shudder. I managed to pull off a smile. "I'm too old to change now. Guess I'll stick to my books and music."

Val rolled her eyes. "Now you're talking like an old woman. You need to get out in the world and start living. Go to England, have it out with her and get it all out of your system. Meet new people, and stop hiding behind that damn wall."

I was beginning to get a little annoyed with her. "Maybe I'm just not that kind of person."

"So what kind of person are you, then?"

I could have told her about my lonely childhood. How I never really knew my father, who was always away in the military. How after his death my mother had ignored me until her own years later. How distant Brandon had been so much of the time.

How hard I found it to bare my soul to anyone.

Instead, I said lightly, "Guess I'm just too independent for my own good."

"Yes, you are." She pouted, managing to look like a petulant little girl. "I want to help you. You're a friend and I always help my friends. Just tell me what you need me to do. You know you can come and live with me until you get things settled."

I smiled at her. I liked her well enough, and I appreciated her generous offer, but I knew our tenuous friendship would not survive the two of us living under the same roof. We'd managed to get along at the club because we'd each had our own job to do, and spent most of the day apart. Thrown together any more than that, we'd drive each other crazy.

She'd tell me what to wear, what to eat and nag me into smothering my face in hideous makeup, the kind that would sink into my wrinkles and make me look ancient. I needed that like I needed a cup of cyanide. "That's so sweet," I murmured. "Thank you, but I should find my own place."

Her face dropped, and I felt as if I'd just stepped on a wounded bird. Cringing inside, I added, "I'll take that help looking for a place, though, if you meant it."

She brightened at once. "Of course I meant it. You know where I am. All you have to do is ask." She looked at her watch. "I have to get back to the club, but call me. Okay?"

I nodded and got to my feet, trying to reconcile all these new decisions with my natural inclination to avoid anything that required upheaval of any kind.

The following morning I awoke with a new sense of purpose. I showered, dressed, put on the coffee then, without giving myself any more time to think, I called the number of the first real estate agency listed in the Yellow Pages.

After talking to the agent, I felt as if I'd just climbed a mountain. It seemed a little unsteady up there, but I'd taken that final step.

A while later Linda Collins introduced herself and marched into my house as if she owned it. With her beauty-spa looks and expensive clothes, she made me feel old and hopelessly outdated. I tried to make up for that with my enthusiasm.

After wandering around the various rooms and giving a very good impression of ignoring my occasional comment, she sat down in the living room and balanced her clipboard on her knee. "So, how much were you thinking of asking for it?" she demanded.

Without giving myself time to think, I named what I immediately felt was an outrageous price.

I expected her to laugh at my ignorance, but instead, she raised her perfectly tweezed eyebrows and said calmly, "Well, you might have to come down a thousand or two, but we'll see what happens. We'll do a neighborhood comparison, that should give us a better idea."

Apparently taking my dazed nod for acceptance, she went on, "Take all the stuff off the walls, put away everything you don't need into drawers. The less clutter you have around the better. Fresh flowers would be nice, and make sure they have a fragrance. Cookies baking in the oven is a nice touch. Gives a house that nice homey feeling. I'll try to give you fair warning when I'm stopping by."

Cookies? I'd never baked in my life. Brandon didn't care for anything that might have expanded his waistline.

Linda shot more questions at me, then I signed a bunch of papers. After promising she'd be back very soon with prospective buyers, she left.

I shut the door behind her and drew a deep breath. I'd done it. I was going to sell the house.

CHAPTER 4

Excited about my newly found confidence, I called Val to tell her. I could hear the excitement in her voice. I half expected her to drop everything and rush right over.

"So you've actually put the house up for sale," she exclaimed. "When are you going to start packing?"

"I was thinking of having the moving people pack for me."

"Are you nuts? I'd never trust my stuff to those idiots. Besides, it will cost a fortune. I hope you can afford lots of insurance."

I couldn't. Now that I came to think of it, I'd probably have to pack everything myself. I let all the air out of my lungs in a long sigh. This independence thing was getting tricky.

"I'll be happy to help you pack."

Now Val sounded wary. Probably expecting me to turn down the offer. I was tempted, but I'd seen enough gift horses' teeth lately. "That would be great. Thanks."

"Sure. It'll be fun. We'll drink wine and play your CDs and party while we're working. By the way, did I tell you I hired another accountant? She's working out pretty well. Not you, of course, but at least it will give me time to come over and help you."

I thanked her and hung up, wondering how much work we'd get done while partying.

My first priority was to pack anything I didn't want strangers to see. The most obvious place to start was Brandon's office. I had just about emptied his file cabinet when I found the large envelope stuffed with mortgage documents.

I flipped through the pages, finding pretty much what I'd expected to see. In spite of what I'd considered an exorbitant price for the house, even if it sold for what I asked, by the time the agent's fees were paid there wouldn't be much left over.

Tucking the last pages back into the envelope, I saw something small and square fall out and land at my feet. It was a photograph, and in it a young woman squinted into the sun while shading her face with one hand. She wore a limp floral dress that barely skimmed her knees and a cardigan wrapped around her shoulders. It wasn't so much the woman that caught my attention, though. It was the cottage behind her.

The sun shone on a thatched roof, latticed windows and an abundance of flowers crowded into a fenced yard. It looked quaint, infinitely charming and exuded a peaceful, quiet solitude. Even as I fell in love with it at first sight, I knew I was looking at *the* cottage. *My cottage.* Which meant the woman standing in front of it had to be *her.*

I stared at her face, at the smile that I knew was for my husband. He must have had this picture for years. I'd fought long and hard to keep an open mind about Brandon's relationship with this woman, but now my fears seemed justified.

My carefully constructed wall of denial finally collapsed. I wanted to scream, to yell, to pound my fists against the wall, to batter his image and hers until they'd been erased from my mind. The thought of them together, laughing, confident their secret was safe, was like a knife in my heart. Now that I knew what she looked like, that vision was all too brutally clear to me.

Jamming the picture into my pants pocket, I thanked heaven Val wasn't there to pummel me with questions and unsolicited advice. I'd have to deal with it sooner or later, but right now I needed to get Brandon's office cleared out before she had a chance to poke around and find more evidence of my late husband's indiscretions.

I worked all afternoon, sorting out papers, shredding what I didn't need, packing away others, while all the time the vision of the cottage smoldered in my mind.

At last I was satisfied I'd taken care of everything. Nothing else incriminating had turned up in Brandon's files, and it was with relief that I shut the door of his office behind me.

Sitting alone in my living room, I took out the picture once more and studied it. The woman's face was fuzzy and I was sure I'd never recognize her if I saw her. Especially after so many years had passed. I squinted harder, striving to see something, anything, that would help me understand.

I don't know how long I sat there, the faded photograph in my hand, while memories crowded my mind. I thought about the day Brandon got his promotion, and how we celebrated over dinner in the Space Needle restaurant.

As the revolving view of the city crawled past our window, we'd raised our glasses of champagne and toasted his success. He'd been more animated that night than I ever remembered, and I was proud of him. He'd worked hard and deserved the success.

I wondered now if he'd called *her* to tell her about the promotion. I racked my brain trying to remember how soon he'd taken a trip to England after that. Had they celebrated there, in some quiet country inn? I imagined the two of them together, laughing across flickering candles and glasses of wine.

Impatient with myself, I tucked the picture away in a drawer and promised myself I wouldn't look at it again. But like a smoker drawn to another pack, I kept going back for one more peek, one more moment of self-torment.

The next few weeks slipped by while I did my best to keep the house "sparkling" clean, as Linda had suggested, for the steady stream of prospective buyers.

Late at night, when the house was dark and quiet and all mine, I thought about the cottage and wrestled with the tug-of-war going on in my mind. There were times when I wanted to go over there and tear out the woman's hair in a screaming catfight. Luckily my horror of making a spectacle of myself in public prevented that option.

I kept telling myself I should put the cottage up for sale, but deep down I knew that once the cottage was sold and the woman who occupied it disappeared, I'd never have the answers I needed so badly. Part of me argued that I didn't want to know. It was the part that did want to know that kept me from calling James.

As the summer died and the first showers of Seattle's rainy season sprinkled the thirsty lawns, I faced the inevitable. Val was right. I would never have true peace of mind until I knew the truth about Brandon's relationship with this woman. Only then could I put the whole mess behind me and get on with my life.

When the house finally sold, I was unprepared. After watching a young couple trailing behind my fast-talking agent, I was sure they hated everything they saw. Linda called a half hour after they left to tell me they'd made an offer.

"It's a good offer," she assured me. "Very close to what I expected. It's up to you, however. You can try a counteroffer, of course, but I think they're pretty firm."

I tried to digest the news, though my brain seemed incapable of working. *This was it.* I say yes now, and it's all over. "Yes," I said, before I could talk myself out of it. "I'll take it."

At first I felt an overwhelming relief that I didn't have to find another mortgage payment. My application for a job with the school district had been put on hold until "something suitable had come up," I'd been informed. I hadn't looked for anything else.

Then reality set in. I called Val. Much as I hated to admit it, I hadn't even begun to pack. I was going to need her help after all.

Val's confident tone reassured me. "I'll come over in a little while. We'll work out a plan of action. While you're waiting for me, mark down apartments in the want ads that appeal to you."

Apartments. Now that I was actually faced with looking for one, all I could think about were the cramped, cold, dark rooms I'd shared with my mother.

I could still hear the music rebounding off the skimpy walls from next door. My mother pounding on the ceiling when heavy, stumbling footsteps threatened to break through. People coming and going, doors slamming, voices shouting — all of it echoed in my head in a waking nightmare of memories.

How would I adjust after living for so long in a house with all this space around me and the quiet solitude I treasured so much?

The cold, sick feeling of dread almost overwhelmed me. I was convinced I'd made a terrible mistake. I should have hung on to the house, managed the mortgage somehow. I could have cut corners, given up the little extras, anything rather than leave the safe haven of my home.

I thought about calling Linda in the hope that it wasn't too late to back out of the deal. I never made the call, of course. Instead I did something I'd never done before. I opened Brandon's cocktail cabinet and took out a half-filled bottle of brandy. I'm no seasoned drinker. By the time Val arrived, my head was buzzing and my tongue had trouble getting out words.

Val took one look at me and plugged in the coffee machine.

My memory of that afternoon is vague, but I remember very clearly the days that followed. The endless packing, sorting and deciding what to keep, what to sell and what to give away. Val insisted we have a garage sale, and I must admit, it gave me a certain satisfaction to see some of Brandon's prized possessions go for a song. He would *not* have appreciated that.

Looking for a place to live was something else. After working out a budget, it was clear that even with a reasonably good salary, any house I felt suitable to rent was out of my range. At least until the cottage sold.

Val insisted on taking me to look at apartments, some of which, I had to admit, were half-decent. They were, however, still apartments, and I felt sick every time I imagined myself sharing walls with noisy strangers.

At the end of one long, fruitless afternoon, Val sat me down in my barren living room. "You have two weeks," she said, "before you have to move out. You should have put the cottage on the market months ago, when you put this one up for sale. You'd have had the money by now and had your pick of where to live. You could even have bought a smaller house."

"I know," I said, aware that this time she was right. "It's too late now."

"Yes, it is." Val looked at me, her eyes clouded with concern. "So what are you going to do?"

"I'll think of something."

"Well, you can always come live with me until you decide what you want to do."

That was the wake-up call, the moment I realized I was out of options. I thanked her anyway, and promised myself I'd make a firm decision by the following morning.

After she left I fished out the photograph once more. As always, the charm and beauty of the tiny cottage stirred a deep-seated longing I didn't fully understand. Half an acre, James had told me. That was a spacious lot. I couldn't see what was on either side of the cottage, but judging from the background, there was nothing behind it but fields and trees.

How wonderful it would be to live somewhere like that, secluded and peaceful in your own private corner of the world. How lucky *she* was to have lived there so long.

Staring at the face of the woman who had caused me so much agonizing, I began to feel ashamed of my stalling. She deserved to know Brandon had died. Whether or not she'd been romantically involved with my husband, she was about to lose her home. I knew how that felt. For once I could afford a tinge of sympathy for her. It would be difficult for her to leave such a paradise.

The next instant I hardened my heart. For all I knew, this woman had stolen my husband's affections and carried on an illicit relationship all these years. Why should my life be shattered and not hers? I called James. It was time to put the cottage on the market.

In his usual brusque way he offered to call the real estate agent in England for me and set things in motion. "Edward Perkins is the man who'll be handling the sale. Would you like him to appoint a lawyer or do you want to go over there and settle things yourself?"

Seconds ticked by while I fought with indecision. Part of me wanted to let someone else deal with the cottage and then try to put it out of my mind. A much bigger part of me knew that would be impossible while there were still so many unanswered questions.

Besides, after all I'd been through, surely I deserved a vacation? Val was right. I had the insurance money, and what better way to spend part of it than on a trip to England. Once the cottage was sold, I'd have plenty of money to tide me over until I landed a job. Before I could change my mind again I said firmly, "You can tell . . . Mr. Perkins was it? Yes, you can tell him I'll be there in a week or so."

James sounded surprised when he asked, "Have you informed Ms. Robbins you're selling the cottage?"

Guilt slapped me square in the chest. "No, I haven't. I thought the estate agent could do that."

James hesitated so long I wondered if he'd heard me. I was about to repeat what I'd said, when he spoke again. "Ah, that's a bit abrupt, don't you think? I mean, it might be better to give the woman a few days' warning before the sales signs go up. Give her a chance to get things squared away."

I fought back the resentment. As far as I was concerned, she deserved no consideration. She certainly hadn't considered me when she'd entertained my husband in that free home he'd so generously given her. "That's fine with me. Just tell the agent to wait a week or two before putting up the signs."

James cleared his throat, a sure signal he was about to say something I didn't want to hear. "You know it might be difficult to sell a house that's renter occupied. You might want to talk to Ms. Robbins and find out if she has any plans to move. After all, a new owner will certainly expect her to pay rent, and since she . . . ah . . . has lived there rent-free until now, she might not be willing to pay for it now, in which case she'll need time to find something more suitable."

It hadn't occurred to me that there might be renter's rights to deal with, and that it might be impossible to get her out of the cottage. Then again, why should I care what she did once the cottage was sold?

Irritable with James for taking her side, I got belligerent. "Have you met this woman?"

His surprise sounded genuine. "Met her? Of course not."

"But you knew about her."

"I knew your husband owned the cottage with a tenant in it. That was all."

"Did you know he kept it a secret from me?"

"I did not. Even if I had, it was not my business to interfere. I advised Brandon on legal matters, that was all."

"Was it legal for him to keep valuable property a secret from his wife?"

"That was a personal decision on his part. Since he ended up leaving you the property in his will, I really don't see the problem."

In other words, his tone implied, I was overreacting. Maybe he was right. There was only one way to find out. I ended the conversation and hung up. I was going to England, and I was going to get the answers to my questions.

Somewhere deep inside me lurked a tiny flicker of hope that this had all been a huge misunderstanding. Until I knew for sure, I would forever torment myself with doubts and unfounded suspicions.

This wasn't something that could be resolved in a letter or a phone call. It would be too easy for the woman to cut me off without a word. I had to deal with her face to face, if I was to get what I needed.

Just to make sure my lack of conviction

wouldn't allow me to back out, I called the airlines and booked a flight to London. Then I called Val. "I'm going to England," I told her. "I'm going over there to sell the cottage and settle things myself."

She was so excited I thought for a moment she was going to suggest coming with me. I was relieved when she said, "I wish I could come, too. I'd love to see her face when you turn up on her doorstep. I'll worry about you all alone over there, but right now I can't leave the club."

"I'll have people to help me over there," I told her. "I'll be just fine." I actually believed it as I hung up, serenely unaware that my long-delayed decision would set off a chain of events that would change my life in ways I could never imagine.

Two weeks later I sat in the window seat of a crowded jumbo jet, trying to convince myself I wasn't in the middle of one of my muddled dreams. The past few days had been a whirlwind of activity and wrenching misgivings as I'd closed the door on my home for the last time.

Red and bronze leaves floated down from the spreading arms of the maple tree in the front yard as I'd driven away, and my heart ached as I'd caught a last glimpse of it just before I'd turned the corner. Right then, all I could remember were the good times. We'd had our share of good times, Brandon and I, even if they had been few and far apart.

Val had helped me put into storage the few things I'd kept, and I'd spent the last two nights in her spacious condo. That alone had been enough to confirm my reservations about living with her for any length of time.

I made up my mind that as soon as I returned, I would use the money from the sale of the cottage to buy myself the first small house I could find.

Val had driven me to the airport, and the last I'd seen of her she was bobbing up and down behind the security gate, waving frantically and yelling last-minute instructions.

I'd never enjoyed air travel. Not that I'd flown that much, anyway. This was the first time, however, that I'd traveled by air on my own. Now that we were actually taxiing down the runway, my insides were clenched as tight as the bolts on the fuselage, and I was quite prepared to hold my breath all the way to London.

Once in the air, I bought two of the little bottles of wine from the flight attendant. By the time I started on the second one, I had begun to float in a pleasant haze of well-being.

The man seated next to me appeared to be about Brandon's age. He seemed harmless enough. Businessman, I suspected, judging from the neat gray suit and silver-blue tie.

He must have noticed my inspection, since he smiled and asked, "Your first trip to Europe?"

"Yes," I admitted, sounding a little breathless — a direct result, no doubt, of having held my breath for so long on takeoff. "I'm on my way to Devon, in England."

"Ah." The man settled back in his chair and lifted what appeared to be a glass of Scotch. "Very nice part of the country."

"You've been there?" Eager to know more about the area, I turned to him.

"Indeed I have."

We spent the next half hour in very pleasant conversation while I learned a great deal about southern England and "the great city of London."

His name was Wes Carter, I found out later, and he was CEO of a big corporation, took frequent business trips to Europe, and lived in San Diego.

I wasn't nearly as forthcoming, telling him

only that I was traveling to England to settle a business matter. The mention of it reminded me of the daunting prospect that lay ahead of me. I tried to imagine how I would feel if the wife of my longtime lover suddenly appeared on my doorstep with the news that he was dead and my home was being sold.

No matter how delicately I handled the situation, it was bound to be devastating for both of us. I wished I'd listened to my instincts and stayed buried in my web of denial. Even as I wished it, I knew I'd come too far to back out now. I was committed to see this through to the bitter end.

Later, as we flew over London and I got my first view of Buckingham Palace and the famous River Thames twisting its way through the ancient city, I wondered what Brandon would have thought if he could see me right then. I hoped that somewhere out there in that vast abyss on the other side, he was watching, filled with remorse for his selfish indiscretions. Racked with guilt and apprehension, I hoped, and aware that I was about to uncover whatever secrets he'd worked so hard to hide.

Chapter 5

My first impression of the English country-side was a hazy blur of vibrant green fields, desolate moors, small modern towns and quaint little villages that made me feel I'd been thrown back in time.

Mostly I dozed in the back of the car I'd hired for the long drive to Devon. By the time the limo pulled up in front of The White Stone Inn, all I wanted was a cup of strong coffee, a quiet room and a soft bed.

The inn had obviously been named for its gleaming white walls that glittered in the midday sun. Beyond the crest of the hill I caught a glimpse of a shimmering dark blue strip of sea beneath a cloudless pale blue sky. The sea air felt mild for late September, and all that talk I'd heard of constant English rain and fog seemed ludicrous in this enchanting setting.

While I waited for the driver to unload my luggage, I looked at the landscape spread out below me. A narrow road wandered through a cluster of buildings that apparently made up the main street of Miles End. At one end the tall steeple of a church seemed to pierce the skyline, and a few uneven rows of houses dotted the area behind it.

I must have been sleeping when I passed through the village. A tingle of excitement woke up my drowsy mind. What fun to explore those crooked streets and intriguing shops! I couldn't wait.

On the heels of that thought came the realization that somewhere down there was the cottage. And *her.* Okay, Eileen Robbins. I had to get used to calling her that, much as I disliked the idea.

My enthusiasm dwindled. Now that I was actually here, I wasn't too thrilled at the thought of confronting the woman. In the next instant I scolded myself. I hadn't come all this way to chicken out. I was determined to be as fair and diplomatic about this mess as possible. There had been far too much secrecy and deceit already.

In the flurry of checking into the inn and getting settled, I managed to forget my worries. I'd been given a charming little room on the top floor. The only drawback as far as I could see was the absence of an elevator, which meant I'd be climbing three flights of stairs. I convinced myself that the exercise would be good for my health, and it would be worth it for the magnificent view of the coastline.

Now that I could see over the hill, I was enchanted by the deep bay and the picturesque harbor. A faint mist hung over the little boats that bobbed around close to shore. A sprinkling of tiny thatched cottages hugged the grassy slopes, and a mass of blossoms set the little square yards ablaze with smudges of dazzling color that reminded me of an artist's palette.

After opening the window, I leaned out to get a better view of my surroundings. Clean, salty air, fresh from the sea, mingled with the heavenly scent of newly cut grass. Below me, an elderly man pedaled with grim determination up the hill on his bicycle, one wheel squeaking in rhythmic protest.

I felt the sun warming my bare arms, and heaved a sigh of pure pleasure. So many times during the hassle of the past few weeks I'd longed for peace and quiet. This tiny village, with its calm streets and pleasant landscape, breathed a serenity that seeped into my body and soul.

I didn't know how long I would stay in Miles End. Much depended on how fast I could deal with *her* and sell the cottage. I couldn't help hoping that my stay would be long enough so that I could enjoy any distractions the tiny village might offer.

I was eager to meet the people, explore the neighborhood, and learn more about this wonderful place my charming companion on the plane had called the English Riviera.

For a fleeting moment I wondered what he was doing, and if he had thought any more about me once we had parted in a flurry of goodbyes and good wishes. Then I forgot him in the fascination of investigating the hotel.

I was somewhat taken aback when I discovered I was expected to share a bathroom with four other rooms on my floor. I was even more upset to note that the spacious bathroom had no shower in the footed tub. Bathing was going to be interesting. Trying to convince myself it was all part of the adventure, I decided to make the best of it. After all, it wouldn't be for long.

My appointment with the real estate agent wasn't until the following morning. I resisted the urge to sleep, and after unpacking my luggage, I made my way down the narrow cobbled street to the village.

The main street meandered between

unique little shops that looked as if they had been plucked from the pages of a Dickens novel. Behind the leaded pane windows a wonderful selection of elegant porcelain ladies and bone-china rabbits peeked out at me from among miniature cottages and lighthouses.

Tearing myself away from all that enchantment, I caught sight of a sign swinging in the stiff breeze from the ocean. On it was painted a bright yellow teapot standing next to a plate of tempting pastries.

It seemed like a haven, beckoning me, especially since I hadn't had anything to eat or drink in hours. I paused in front of a wooden door, feeling as if I were about to enter Snow White's cottage.

As I stepped inside, a bell jangled angrily above my head. The inside of the tearoom looked even more like a scene from Disney. A dozen or so little square tables had been crammed into a space no bigger than my living room. A wide ledge ran around the walls, bearing the weight of brass cooking pots, copper kettles and huge china jugs.

It was the heavenly fragrance of fresh-baked bread, however, that convinced me to move farther into the room, wondering why this amazing place wasn't jammed with customers.

"Can I help you?"

The raspy voice had come from behind me, and I swung around. The chunky woman facing me wore a floral dress covered with a white apron, and soiled red velvet slippers. A pair of granny glasses sat on the end of her nose and she peered over them, studying me with frank curiosity.

Being the target of such a formidable scrutiny was uncomfortable, and I had second thoughts about sitting down. "Are you open for business?" I asked, half-expecting the woman would tell me to come back later.

"I am. Take a seat. You've got plenty of choice." She waved a flabby arm at the tables.

"Thank you." I sank down on the nearest chair and laid my purse on the vacant one next to me. "I'd like a pot of tea and a Danish."

The woman's dark eyes narrowed in curiosity. "You're American, aren't you?"

I nodded with a smile.

"On holiday, are you?"

The woman seemed in no hurry to get my order, and her direct questions began to make me uncomfortable. I wasn't used to this small-town cosiness with strangers. "As a matter of fact I'm here on business." I picked up the well-thumbed menu and studied it in the hopes of discouraging any more conversation.

My hostess was not easily put off. "Not much business going on around here. Mostly tourist stuff. What sort of business you in, then?"

I hoped my tone would warn her I didn't like her prying. "I'm here to sell some property. A cottage to be exact."

Ignoring the hint, her voice rose. "Oh, you're here to sell the Hodges' cottage. I heard it was going up for sale."

Thoroughly impatient now, I shook my head. "No, not that one. I'm in rather a hurry. Could I get my order, please?"

"Oh, of course. Be back in a jiff."

She waddled off in the direction of the kitchen and I slumped down on my chair. My head felt as if it had separated from my shoulders. The lack of sleep had caught up with me. I did a mental calculation. It had been more than twenty-four hours since I'd woken up in Seattle. I hoped the tea would keep me awake me long enough to get back to the hotel.

The waitress returned a short time later with a tray bearing a miniature teapot, milk jug and sugar bowl, an exquisite bone-china cup and saucer, and two large pastries. She set the tray in front of me and folded her arms. "You sure it's not the Hodges' cottage? The one on Marsh Lane?"

That rang a bell. "Well, yes, it is in Marsh Lane, but it's not that cottage. It must be another one."

The woman smiled. "There's only one cottage in Marsh Lane, dearie. That's the Hodges' cottage. Mr. Perkins, the estate agent was in here two days ago. He told me the American owner was coming here to sell the place." Her smile faded and her sigh seemed to echo like the wind before a storm. "I don't know what the Hodges will do, and that's a fact, with three little ones and all." With that she turned and bustled off, leaving me in a haze of confusion.

Little ones? The Hodges? In my cottage? Hot on the heels of those baffling thoughts came another one. If this woman knew that the cottage was being sold, that meant Eileen Robbins probably knew as well. James must have assumed I'd been in touch with her, or had simply neglected to warn the real estate agent to keep the sale a secret until I'd talked to her. Either way, by now she most likely knew the bad news.

At first I felt a surge of relief that I hadn't had to break it to her myself, after all. Guilt quickly followed. It couldn't have been pleasant for her, hearing it that way. I'd heard about small-town grapevines but hadn't dreamed they could be so efficient. I hoped Edward Perkins had been tactful.

That brought me back to the waitress's weird comments. Who were the Hodges? Did Eileen Robbins have people living with her in the cottage? Surely Brandon wouldn't have wanted that? Perhaps he didn't know. Now what was I going to do? How was I going to deal with this new turn of events?

My mind continued to whirl in useless circles, while I fought a rising sense of confusion. I should never have come. I should have let a lawyer deal with it all and hang the cost.

I needed to get back to the hotel and lie down. My hunger had all but disappeared, but I hated to waste the luscious pastries. They were as light and flaky as they looked, although I washed them down with the strong, scalding tea without any real enjoyment of the treat.

The bill still lay on the tray, and I looked at it, unable to understand the figure at the bottom. I'd changed some dollars into British currency at the airport, and I threw down what I thought was an appropriate amount and scrambled for the door.

I thought I heard the waitress call out

something, but I was in no mood for any more surprises. I wanted to lie down in a quiet room, and let the weariness take me into sweet oblivion. Maybe then it would all make sense.

In my rush to escape the urgent voice of the woman behind me, I shoved the door open and barged out onto the street. I didn't see the man outside until I'd charged right into him. I gave him a hefty blow with my purse right in the stomach.

Hearing his agonized grunt, I took a leap backward that would have made Val proud. Words tumbled from my mouth. "I'm real sorry . . . I didn't see you . . . I hope I didn't hurt you . . . I —"

"Hold on, hold on." His voice sounded ragged, but he gave me an expansive grin. "I'm still breathing. I imagine I'll survive."

Maybe it was the sight of that appealing grin, the kindness in his clear blue gaze. Maybe it was losing Brandon, the upheaval of the past month, the shock of learning my life had been a lie, the mounting complications, the jet lag.

Whatever it was, it all caught up with me in one huge rush. Afraid I was about to cry or throw up or something, I backed away, one hand over my mouth. I saw concern wipe the man's smile away and felt like an idiot. Without another word I turned and fled down the street.

He called out after me, but all I wanted was to escape from him, from this place full of riddles and nasty surprises. I wanted to go back to my nice safe home in Seattle, shut the door and forget there ever was a cottage. *Damn Brandon. Damn Eileen Robbins. Damn everyone and everything. Damn, damn, damn.*

My sound, dreamless sleep went a long way toward helping me feel better, and by the time I'd walked down to the estate agent's office the next morning, I felt a little more in control of my emotions.

Edward Perkins was a dapper little man with hardly any hair and a nervous habit of twitching his nose. He sat behind a cluttered desk that defied any hope of organization. The office stank of tobacco smoke, and my still-delicate stomach rebelled at the sight of crushed cigarette butts filling the ashtray at the agent's elbow.

He greeted me with a courtesy that barely disguised his curiosity. "Mr. Starrett told me you were coming," he said, his voice so high-pitched it could have been a woman's.

And he'd wasted no time in spreading the news, I thought, with more than a spark of resentment. Maybe grapevines were acceptable in these parts, but I considered it highly unprofessional of him to discuss my personal business affairs with strangers.

He peered at me over the top of glasses that appeared to have trouble clinging to his nose. "I trust you had a good trip over the pond?"

"Very nice, thank you."

"Good, good. Glad to hear it." He rubbed his hands together, "Now, about this business of selling the cottage —"

I interrupted him. "Excuse me, Mr. Perkins. There's just one thing I'd like to know before we start."

He looked at me as if I'd stated I was about to blow up the building. "Well, I don't know that I can —"

"Who are the Hodges?"

His look of astonishment would have been comical if I'd been less strung out with tension. "I beg your pardon?"

"A woman I met yesterday mentioned someone named Hodges and their three children. I'd like to know who these people are and what they are doing in my cottage."

The agent tugged at the greasy-looking tie at his neck. His air of superiority vanished completely as he stammered, "But I thought you knew. The Hodges live there."

So, my suspicions had been well-founded. "They live with Eileen Robbins?"

"Oh!" His face cleared. "I can see where the confusion comes in. Eileen lived in the cottage until she died several years ago."

Stunned, I stared at him. *Eileen Robbins, the woman with all the answers, was dead?* I'd come all that way for nothing. The realization that I'd never know the truth clutched my heart like a cold hand.

Struggling to overcome the bitter disappointment, I realized I still had a problem. "So who are these people living there now? Who gave them permission to live there?"

"Why, your husband, Mr. Maitland, did, of course."

There was no *of course* about it. I was floundering again in confusion. What did the Hodges have to do with Brandon?

Edward Perkins fidgeted with the papers in front of him, then answered my unspoken question. "You see, Mrs. Maitland, well . . . ah . . . Gillian Hodge is Eileen's daughter."

I didn't see, of course. Not yet. "So Gillian Hodge is now living in the cottage with her husband?"

Perkins nodded, obviously relieved that I'd finally gotten it. "Right. Ned's the name. Nice chap. Oh, and then there's their three youngsters, of course. Craig, Sheila and

Robbie. Craig's the oldest. He's eight, I believe."

How very generous of my husband, I thought bitterly, to allow his lover's family to live in the cottage. So Eileen had been married after all. I wondered if her husband knew about Brandon. Maybe that's why she lived in the cottage. Her husband must have found out about Brandon and divorced her.

The tangle in my head was getting worse. I needed this whole thing straightened out and I needed it now. "I want to see the cottage," I said abruptly. "Now. Today."

Edward Perkins frowned. "Oh, I don't think that would be wise. Perhaps another time, when I can let Mrs. Hodge know you're coming?"

"Why can't you call her?" I gestured at the black squat phone on his desk.

"Well, I don't like to just ring up and say we're on our way. Some people like to have time to tidy up a bit for visitors. Especially when they have kiddies."

I didn't care about other people. I only cared about the people occupying my cottage. Wondering when I had become so possessive of it, I said loudly, "I'm sorry, but I really must insist."

His face grew cold, and he snapped the papers together and thrust them into a file.

"Very well. I just hope Mrs. Hodge won't be too put out."

She couldn't be nearly as put out as I was. "Well, we'll just have to take that chance," I said crisply, and waited for him to pick up the phone.

I listened to him explaining that I was anxious to see the cottage, practically pleading with the woman to allow us to visit. Burning with resentment, I wanted to snatch the phone from his hand and tell this intruder that she was trespassing on my property and I'd look at it any time I damn well wanted.

Of course I couldn't do that. For one thing, I had no idea exactly what the rights were for people occupying a house, even if they weren't paying rent. Especially if Brandon had given his permission for them to do so.

Finally Edward Perkins got the answer he wanted. "She wasn't too happy about it, so I suggest we make it brief," he said, as he headed for the door.

I didn't say so aloud, but I wasn't going to leave until I was good and ready. Whether Mrs. Hodge was happy or not. This family was living on property that I owned, without any visible payment of any kind, and I was bound and determined to put an end to this amazing charity my husband had been handing out, for whatever reason I was going to find out. Even if it wasn't what I wanted to hear.

I followed the disgruntled man out to his car, a sleek silver vehicle that seemed totally out of place in the antiquated street. He said little to me on the way there, and I tried to relax as we headed for a thicket of trees that lay a short distance from the town.

A few minutes later we turned into a lane and bumped to a halt outside a thick, tall hedge. Edward Perkins cut the engine and unsnapped his seat belt. "Here we are," he announced unnecessarily.

My stomach danced with apprehension. I'd never been good at confrontation. Even with Brandon I'd done my best to avoid antagonizing him, often sacrificing my own wishes for his in order to keep the peace.

I felt my lips pinching with the stress as I climbed out of the car. *Get in there, get it over with, and get out,* I told myself. The sooner I did that, the sooner I could be on my way back to Seattle. The fact that I no longer had a home waiting for me there didn't seem to matter. I wanted to be back on familiar ground, with familiar faces and places surrounding me.

I missed Val. I missed Brandon. For the

first time in many weeks, I wanted my old life back.

CHAPTER 6

That particular sentiment vanished the second the door opened to reveal a woman framed in the doorway.

At first glance she appeared to be just a few years younger than me. As I moved forward, I realized she was closer to thirty. Her hair had been scraped back and tied with a black ribbon, and her skin was clear of makeup. She wore black socks but no shoes, and her crumpled shirt had seen better days.

One hand clutched the doorframe while the other rested on her hip in a defiant pose that seemed oddly familiar. Warning signals sprinted down my back. "I haven't cleared up," she announced, staring at me as if daring me to protest.

"I'm sure Mrs. Maitland understands," Perkins twittered.

"Of course," I murmured.

"Well, you'd better come in, then." She

stood back and waved a hand at the interior of the cottage.

Perkins stood back and allowed me to enter first. A blue couch and two matching armchairs fought for space with a large dresser, a television set and three small tables scattered in between. A bag sat on the couch with knitting needles sticking out of it, and a pair of sneakers lay by the front door.

Mrs. Hodge bent to pick them up, than straightened. "If you want a cup of tea I can put the kettle on," she offered, though with enough reluctance to discourage us from accepting.

"That won't be necessary, thank you very much," Perkins answered for me. "We won't be taking up too much of your time. Mrs. Maitland wanted a peep at the cottage before she puts it up for sale, that's all. Isn't that right, Mrs. Maitland?"

"Well, there's not much to see." Mrs. Hodge pointed across the room to a hallway. "The kitchen's down there, and the bed-rooms are upstairs."

Right then, much as I'd longed to explore the cottage, all I wanted was answers. "Do you mind if I sit down?" Without waiting for a reply, I chose an armchair. The springs sank under my weight and squeaked in protest.

Both Mrs. Hodge and Perkins stared at me as if I'd committed a mortal sin. "I thought you wanted to look over the house," the agent said, shooting an apologetic glance in the other woman's direction.

"What I want," I said, "is to find out exactly what your arrangements were with my husband."

Mrs. Hodge opened her mouth to answer, but at that moment a door opened somewhere in the back of the house and raised voices of children echoed down the hallway.

Mrs. Hodge glanced at the clock. "It's the children home for lunch," she muttered. "I won't be a minute."

I wondered why the children weren't in school, then belatedly realized it was Saturday. I'd lost a day somewhere on my trip across the ocean.

I could hear Mrs. Hodge talking in a low voice, then the high-pitched voice of a child answered her. "All the way from America? Did she sail in a boat?"

Again Mrs. Hodge muttered something.

"I wanna see her!"

"You stay right here!"

There followed a scuffling sound, then footsteps pounded down the hallway. A was bothering to tell her such an intimate detail about the man who had so cruelly deceived me. "It made him sterile."

The fleeting pity in her eyes warned me. Even so I was unprepared when she said, "I'm only twenty-seven."

I did the calculation and sank down on the chair. The front door opened and Perkins bustled back in, carrying a file under his arm. He said something, but I was past comprehending. He took one look at me and added, "Perhaps we'd better do this another time."

Somehow I pushed myself out of the chair and made it to the door. I didn't care what happened to the cottage, or the family who lived in it. I didn't even care what happened to me. All I knew was that Brandon had told me the most heartless lie of all. Knowing how much I'd wanted a child, he'd deceived me and denied me the most important wish of my life.

Perhaps, in time, I could have forgiven him the rest of it.

Lots of men had affairs, and marriages survived in spite of it. But this — this outrage — was something I could never forgive. For the first time since I'd learned about the existence of the cottage, I truly hated my dead husband.

small boy burst into the room, coming to an abrupt halt as his dark eyes met mine.

He was about five years old and the image of his mother, with brown hair that curled around his ears and an engaging smile that seemed to light up his whole face. Again I was struck by an odd sense of familiarity as I smiled back.

"Hi," I said. "My name is Marjorie. What's yours?"

"Robbie." He came closer, his head tilted on one side. "Mummy says you're taking the house away from us."

I could feel Perkins's disapproving stare on me as I answered. "No, honey, I'm not going to take the house away from you. Someone else will be owning it, that's all."

"And what's supposed to happen to us, then?" Mrs. Hodge's voice said from the doorway.

I raised my head and met her accusing glare. "I imagine the new owner will expect you to pay rent," I said, conscious of my cool tone.

"Sheila says you're my grandma," Robbie announced.

I thought how cute that was and gave the adorable child another smile. I was about to set him straight, but his mother's sharp voice cut across the room.

"Shut *up, Robbie.* Go and finish your lunch. *Now.*"

Something about the urgency of her voice caught my attention. I looked up, just as the little boy said, "Sheila says that Grandpa's gone to heaven."

Even then, I might have accepted his words as those of a confused little boy, had it not been for the expression on his mother's face. Her dismay far outweighed the innocent misunderstanding of a child.

It was then that I finally understood. The reason I'd felt that odd sense of familiarity. It was in the eyes, the tilt of the head, the curve of the lips. I could see it in her and in the small boy who now stood silent and uneasy, one thumb jammed in his mouth.

We sat there, Mrs. Hodge and I, in that frigid silence, just staring at each other, until Perkins coughed, and muttered, "I've . . . ah . . . left some papers in the car. I'll just go and get them . . . ah . . . yes . . ."

He practically ran from the room. His hasty exit broke the awkward trance, and Mrs. Hodge spoke sharply to her son. "Robbie, go back to the kitchen this second. Tell your sister to give you a piece of cake and wait there until I come."

Something in her tone must have penetrated, as Robbie fled down the hallway without another word.

I got to my feet, and as I did so, I felt as if some strange force pulled me out of the room, backward and at great speed. I clung to the arm of the chair, and slowly everything swam into focus again.

I looked at Gillian Hodge, and said with quiet conviction, "You're Brandon's daughter."

Her answer brought what little was left of my past marriage tumbling to the ground. "Yes," she said. "Brandon Maitland was my father."

For several seconds the silence seemed to hang between us like a thick, dark curtain.

"I wasn't going to tell you," Gillian said, moving farther into the room. "But then everyone else knows, so you'd have heard about it sooner or later."

My mind still groping to understand, I fought to keep my voice steady. "He must have been very young. . . ."

She frowned. "It was a long time ago."

"Before he had the mumps."

"Mumps?"

I didn't blame her for looking so bewildered. I was floundering in the dark as well, trying to understand. "Brandon had the mumps when he was fifteen," I said, wondering in some small part of my mind why I

Perkins said nothing as he drove me back to the hotel, but his silence only intensified my resentment. I was shaking with fury by the time I clambered out of the car. I mumbled something about calling him and ran up the steps of the hotel. I hurried through the lobby, past the surprised face of the clerk and didn't stop until I was inside my room with the door locked securely behind me.

Strangely enough, I was just too angry to cry. I threw my purse down on the bed and stalked to the window. Throwing it open, I leaned out and gulped huge, deep mouthfuls of air. My entire body trembled from head to toe, and my fingers curled into fists on the windowsill. It was just as well Brandon was dead, because right at that moment, I fully believed I was capable of murder.

The thought brought me quickly to my senses. I sank on the bed and tried to rein in my chaotic thoughts. Only then did the realization hit me with full force. I had longed for a family. Now I had one. Gillian Hodge was my stepdaughter.

I sat there for a long time, trying to decide what to do next. I needed to talk to Gillian again. There were still so many unanswered questions. But not now. Not yet. The wounds were far too fresh. I needed time to absorb the blows.

There was the sale of the cottage to deal with, made so much more complicated now that I knew the truth about its occupants. I needed a lawyer, I decided. James would be of no help at all. I'd have to ask Perkins to recommend someone. The thought of dealing with that irritating little man again was so disagreeable I decided to put it all off until tomorrow.

The rest of the day I would spend by myself, and try to recover some sort of composure. Maybe then I'd feel strong enough to face whatever else fate had ready to throw at me.

Aware that I'd be making matters worse by shutting myself up alone in that room, I forced myself to go back down the stairs and out of the front door.

The clerk greeted me as I went by the desk, and not trusting my voice to speak just yet, I answered with a wave of my hand.

Once outside I began to feel a little more human. Thick white clouds scurried across the sky, blotting out the sun as I walked once more down the main street of the village.

The sea breeze chilled my bare arms, and belatedly I realized I should have brought a jacket with me. I'd forgotten how quickly the weather could change at the coast.

This time I went inside the antique shop, in the hopes that browsing among fascinating relics from the past would help me escape the present for a while.

It felt a little like stepping into a damp, dark cave, with the musty smell of a room that had been closed off for too long. I had to blink to adjust my vision, and a movement near the rear of the shop caught my eye.

The woman who hobbled toward me appeared to be older than the objects displayed on her shelves. The hem of her floral dress touched the floor, and she leaned heavily on a cane. Strangely, however, she wore no glasses, and she blinked at me with bright, beady eyes that reminded me of an inquisitive bird. In a startling strong voice she demanded, "Were you looking for something special?"

"Oh, no, thank you," I hurried to assure her. "I was just browsing." I glanced around at the packed shelves. "You have some wonderful antiques here."

I looked back at her, to find her staring hard at me. Gillian's words echoed in my mind. *But then everyone else knows, so you'd have heard it sooner or later.*

Just how many people was *everyone*, I wondered. Did this woman know how my husband had betrayed me, lied to me, deprived me of the child I had ached to hold in my arms? Was that pity I saw in her eyes, or was she secretly laughing at my stupidity?

Obeying the desperate urge to get out of there, I muttered my thanks and hurtled into the street. Once more I almost collided with a man. Only this time he managed to sidestep my assault and I whizzed past him. I recognized him the second I brushed by his shoulder. Mortified, I halted and twisted around to face him.

He stood smiling at me, the wind whipping a lock of hair across his forehead. "Hello again. We've got to stop meeting like this."

An answering smile tugged at my lips. "We're getting better. I missed you this time."

"Thanks to my spectacular soft-shoe shuffle." He did a little dance sideways. "Didn't know you were dealing with such an accomplished performer, did you."

"I'm sorry, I . . ."

"Hey, no need to apologize." He narrowed his eyes. "You're not going to dash off again, are you?"

Feeling absurdly shy for some reason, I shook my head.

"Thank goodness." He patted a hand over his heart. "For a while there I thought my ugly mug was scaring you off."

Now that I had a good look at him, I thought he was anything but ugly. He had the kind of open face that elicited trust — a wide, engaging grin, eyes that gleamed with humor, a frank, direct gaze that made me feel he was genuinely interested in what I had to say.

I felt my tension begin to ease as I said, "I'm sorry about yesterday. Jet lag, I guess. I hope you didn't take it personally."

"Ah." He nodded. "Well, that explains it." He lifted his wrist and peered at a chunky silver watch. "I was just on my way to grab a spot of lunch. Care to join me?"

He must have sensed my immediate withdrawal. He waved a hand at the street behind me. "The Tea Parlor . . . just up the road. Gladys makes a smashing Cornish pastie."

I raised my eyebrows. "Pastie?"

"Meat and potatoes inside a pastry envelope." He looked shocked. "Don't tell me you've never tasted one! You've never lived!" To my intense discomfort, he took hold of my arm. "Come on, I'll treat you. It's the least I can do after trying to trip you up two days in a row."

If I hadn't been so disturbed by his commandeering attitude, I'd have reminded him it was I who had barged into him. As it was, I was so busy collecting my composure I failed to realize I'd arrived back in the tea shop I'd fled from a day earlier.

Not only that, the prying woman in the velvet slippers advanced toward us, her face creased in a smile. This, I assumed, was Gladys, the baker of the acclaimed Cornish pastie.

"I'm so glad you came back," she said, her focus zooming in on our linked arms. "You left too much money on the table yesterday. I was wondering how to get it back to you."

Feeling my cheeks growing warm, I pulled my arm free and moved away from my benefactor's side. "That's all right. Keep it as a tip."

Gladys shook her head and dug into the pocket of her apron. "No, dearie, I don't take advantage of visitors. Here." She thrust a couple of crumpled bills into my unwilling hand. "Though, if you want to spend it in here I won't say no."

"She wants to try your pasties, Glad." The man at my side nudged my arm. "I've been telling her how brilliant they are."

Gladys's face glowed with pride. "Don't take no notice of Dan, dearie. A big tease he is, all right." She punched him lightly in the chest. "Go on with you, then. Get the lady a seat. Where's your bloomin' manners?"

Dan grinned. "Go and warm up those pasties then, there's a luv." Once more he took my arm, and led me to a corner table next to the window. "Tea? A glass of wine? Or would you rather have a beer?"

Still wondering how on earth I'd ended up having lunch with a complete stranger, I sat down in the chair he'd pulled out for me. "I'd like some iced tea, please."

"I'll see what Gladys can do." He wandered off in the direction of the kitchen, giving me a welcome few minutes to catch my breath. I was hungry again, I realized. It had to be that heavenly aroma of freshly baked bread.

The doorbell jangled as a couple of elderly women entered. Without waiting for Gladys to seat them, they made their way to a table across the room, sending me blatant stares of curiosity as they passed my table. I felt as if I were on display in a zoo, for everyone to gawk at in curious wonder.

My companion came back to the table,

and I could feel the stares of the other customers burning into my back. It didn't help when he gave me a formal bow and held out his hand. "We haven't been properly introduced," he announced, without troubling to lower his voice. "I'm Dan Connelly, owner and proprietor of Connelly's Boating Supplies, and a regular customer here at The Parlor."

"Marjorie Maitland." I took his hand and returned his strong handshake. "I'm here on business."

Dan nodded as he sat down. "Glad told me you were selling the Hodges' cottage."

A spark of resentment spoiled my pleasant mood. Did everyone in this town discuss everyone's business so freely? I wanted to inform him that it was my cottage, not the Hodges', but knowing that would sound petty I held my tongue.

"Have you met them yet?" Dan's frank gaze rested on my face and I knew some of my bitterness must have been visible. I wondered then how much he knew, how much Gladys knew, how much the women across the room and the woman in the antique shop knew. In that moment I had never felt so exposed in all my life.

"I've met Gillian Hodge and her little boy, Robbie," I said, hoping my voice didn't give away my tension.

"Nice people." He paused, then added, "I don't suppose you've had time for seeing the sights yet."

I looked at him in surprise. In a village this size I couldn't imagine what else there was to see other than the harbor and the quaint, narrow main street. "There are sights?"

"Well, by American standards I suppose they're not much, but we're rather fond of them."

I was immediately embarrassed. "I'm sorry, I didn't mean to sound arrogant. It was just that the town is so small and I thought . . ." I let my voice trail off, aware I was simply making things worse.

His smile was tinged with sympathy, though I couldn't imagine why. He leaned forward and lowered his voice. "You say you're sorry a lot, don't you."

I stared at him. I supposed I had apologized a few times in the short time I'd known him. It was on the tip of my tongue to say I was sorry again, but I bit it back.

He patted my hand, making the nerves in my arm jump. "It's all right. I forgive you."

While I was still trying to figure out exactly what he meant by that, he added, "About the sights. We have a lighthouse, though it's a bit run-down. Still, it's been there over a hundred years, and I hear Yanks love anything that's old."

I suspected he was teasing me again, and I refused to rise to the bait. "I'd love to take a look at it. Where is it?"

"Up the coast a bit. You'd need a car. Then there's Cairnmouth Castle. That's even more ancient."

My eyes widened at this. "There's a castle here?"

I listened, fascinated, as Dan launched into a history of Miles End and the surrounding area.

A young girl with startling bright red hair and a ring stabbed through her nose brought the pasties, which I had to admit, with their onion flavor and tender morsels of beef, lived up to Dan's glowing recommendation. The iced tea on the other hand tasted bitter, and the two ice cubes floating around in the glass left the dark brown liquid lukewarm.

I watched Dan take a swallow of his beer and wished I'd followed his example. It occurred to me at the same moment that in spite of our brief acquaintance, I felt more at ease with him than any other man I'd met. Including my late husband.

I was still dealing with that stunning

realization when Dan said, "Gladys told me you lost your husband a few months ago."

I nodded, wondering again how much he knew.

"I'm sorry. It must be hard for you, dealing with all this on your own."

I decided to give him the benefit of the doubt and assume he was talking about the sale of the cottage. "I'm getting used to it."

"Well, if you need advice or just someone to talk to, Glad's got a broad shoulder and she's always here."

The sympathy in his face was almost my undoing. I murmured my thanks, and directed my attention out the window.

The sound of his chair scraping back brought my head around.

"Well, I hate to eat and run, but duty calls." He stood smiling down at me, and I started to get up, but he stopped me with a raised hand. "No, stay here and finish your tea." He started to leave, then paused to look back at me. "I enjoyed the company and our chat."

"Me, too. Thanks for lunch."

"My pleasure. And by the way, my shoulder's pretty broad, too." Without waiting for an answer, he strode to the door and disappeared.

Chapter 7

I sat at that table for a long time after Dan left, reluctant to leave my secure little corner. I watched the withered leaves scurrying and dancing in the wind across the sidewalk. I knew it would be chilly out there without my jacket, and I wasn't looking forward to the walk back to the hotel.

A few more customers had entered since I'd first sat down, but now most of them had gone, including the two curious women from across the room. The last two, a young couple obviously on their honeymoon, left arm in arm, absorbed in each other. I watched them wander off down the street, wondering how it must feel to be that much in love.

There's nothing more emotionally painful than the ache of regret and I was full of it as I watched the happy couple gazing at each other with such total adoration. Twenty-seven years of my life living a lie.

What a terrible waste.

When someone spoke at my side, I jumped, startled out of bleak thoughts. Gladys stood there, her arms crossed, her expression reminding me of Dan's sympathetic eyes. "Like another glass of that iced tea, would you?"

I shook my head. "Thanks, but I should go. I've sat here too long as it is."

To my surprise, she wedged herself behind the table in the chair Dan had vacated. "Stay and have a pot of tea with me. Janice is getting it for us."

Janice, I assumed, was the young girl who'd waited on us earlier. I didn't want to sit and talk to this busybody, who probably knew more about me and my business than I did myself. While I was trying to think of a polite way to leave, however, the sullen Janice marched up to us and dumped a loaded tray onto our table.

"I'm going now," she announced, fluffed her tufted hair with one heavily ringed hand and flounced out the door.

Gladys clicked her tongue and reached for the teacups. Turning them up the right way in their saucers, she muttered, "Can't get good help anywhere these days. These young girls don't like taking orders. Think they know it all, they do."

I didn't quite know how to respond to this, so I kept quiet.

Gladys lifted the lid from the tiny silver bowl. "Sugar?"

"No, thank you." I accepted the steaming cup and saucer and set it down in front of me.

"Nice that you met Dan." Gladys stirred sugar into her tea, then laid the spoon back in the saucer with a clatter. "He's a good sort, that one."

Thankful I wasn't the subject of the conversation, I seized the opportunity to find out more about him. "He seems very nice. He told me he owns a boating supplies store."

"That he does. Don't know for how much longer, though." Gladys picked up the creased menu and starting fanning her face, although the room had cooled down considerably now that the customers had left. "Business is falling off for him. People like the big towns better. Even our youngsters are off to the city as soon as they're out of school. Don't want to work in the fields anymore."

I was about to comment when she added, "That's what Ned Hodge does. Works on a farm. Not much money doing that."

A hollow feeling crept into my stomach.

Certain that she was trying to tell me something, I said carefully, "I met Mrs. Hodge and her youngest son, Robbie, this morning."

"Did you now." The sharp brown eyes studied me. "She told you, didn't she."

There was no point in pretending I didn't know what she meant. I nodded.

"Must have been quite a shock."

"Yes, it was."

"Gillian worried about it, you know. Soon as she heard you were coming over to sell the cottage, she came and asked me what she should do. She knew you didn't know, you see. About her and the kiddies, I mean."

"And that's why you tried to warn me yesterday," I said, suddenly understanding.

"Well, I couldn't say much, could I. After all, it was none of my business." Gladys slurped her tea, then set the cup down again. "I thought if I mentioned the kiddies you'd ask Mr. Perkins about them and it wouldn't be quite such a shock."

I'd misjudged the woman. She hadn't been prying, she'd been trying to prepare me. "Thank you," I said.

Gladys reached across the table and patted my arm. "Look, I know what a nasty shock it must have been. To find out your husband was supporting another family and never told you nothing about it. I'm sorry, dearie. If you want to talk about it, well I've got nothing to do for an hour or so. I'm a good listener."

I don't know if it was because of her attempt to soften the blow yesterday, or the genuine concern I saw in her eyes. Maybe it was the motherly figure, the gentle tone, or simply the fact that I had no one else to confide in. In any case, I found myself telling her everything.

I told her how much I'd wanted a child, and the lousy way Brandon had deceived me. I told her about our marriage, and the gulf between us I hadn't realized was there until he'd died.

The words tumbled from me in a way that had never happened before. It seemed as if once I'd started, I simply couldn't stop. As I talked, the hard knot that had plagued my stomach all day gradually began to ease.

"Some men are hard to love," Gladys said, when I finally stopped talking. "Doesn't mean he didn't love you in his way."

"How could he lie to me like that if he loved me?" My hand trembled as I lifted my cup to my lips.

"He stayed married to you, didn't he?" Gladys brushed at the front of her apron with her stubby fingers. "He must have had some feelings for you to stay with you all those years."

I shook my head in bewilderment. "Why? Why didn't he marry Eileen and live here with her and Gillian?"

Gladys pursed her lips. "That's something only he and Eileen knew. Unless she told Gillian, in which case, you'll have to ask her."

"I don't think I can talk to Gillian about this. After all, Eileen was her mother."

"And you're her stepmother," Gladys said firmly. "Whether Gillian likes it or not, you have a right to know the truth. You say you always wanted a family. Well, there's three little kiddies out there who need a grandmother. Seems to me you could do a lot of good by talking to Gillian and getting to know her."

I plucked at the tablecloth and pleated the edge of it between my fingers. "She didn't seem very friendly."

"She'll come around." In spite of my shake of the head, Gladys refilled my cup. "She's had a lot of time to build up her bitterness over her daddy deserting her and her mother like that. They had a rough time of it for a long time, you know. If it hadn't been for your husband buying them the cottage I hate to think what would have happened to them. It was hard on Eileen, having to work and take care of a little one all by herself."

"She didn't have family she could ask for help?"

"Eileen fell out with her family when she got pregnant with Gillian. They wouldn't have nothing to do with her."

Much to my surprise, I felt a twinge of sympathy. I hadn't considered the fact that Brandon had deserted her and his child, which I suppose he had. It seemed he had betrayed both of us. My anger against him deepened.

"Gillian feels you took him away from them, you see," Gladys added. "I suppose she blames you for the rotten life she had growing up."

I stared at her, at a complete loss for words. All this time I had considered myself the injured party, having discovered there was another woman in my husband's life. To realize that I was seen as the other woman was a nasty shock. "That's so unfair," I said, unable to keep the anger out of my voice. "I didn't meet Brandon until after all this happened."

"There ain't much fair when it comes to men and women." Gladys stirred her tea a little too vigorously and some of it slopped over into her saucer. "Take me, for instance. Thirty-two years I gave to the bugger I married, and what thanks do I get? He runs off with a woman half his age. Last I heard he had three little kiddies to take care of and jolly well serve him right, I say."

"I'm sorry," I muttered, still too immersed in my own indignation to be genuinely sympathetic.

"Yeah, well, it left me in the lurch, didn't it. Fifty-two I was when I took over the lease on this place." She waved a hand at the empty room. "Worked day and night to build it up. Near on killed me, it did."

I nodded, hearing the words without paying attention to their meaning. Gillian resented me. *Me.* I was the one who had been deceived, and deprived of my fondest dream. What right did she have to resent me? She had three children and a husband. I had nothing. No one.

"I have to go," I said, rising to my feet.

Gladys looked surprised. "Aren't you going to finish your tea?"

"No, thank you. I forgot . . . I have to make a call." I unhooked the strap of my purse from the back of the chair and shoved it onto my shoulder. "Thank you for the tea, and for the conversation. It was very enlightening."

Gladys's shrewd expression challenged me. "Try to understand how Gillian feels. I know it's hard, but you two need each other. It would be a shame to turn your back on the only family you'll ever have. After all, your husband left you the cottage, didn't he. If he hadn't you'd never have known about them. Maybe he wanted you and Gillian to get to know each other, so you wouldn't be alone."

I dismissed that with another shake of my head. "It's more likely he wanted a clear conscience. In any case, he chose a cruel way to come clean about his secret life."

Gladys shrugged. "He could have meant to tell you, but died before he could find a good time to do it."

I was in no mood to give Brandon the benefit of the doubt. In the space of two days I'd learned far more about my husband than I'd even begun to imagine. I wanted to bury my head in a soft pillow and blot out the lies, the unjustified resentment directed against me by my husband's illegitimate daughter. I wanted to go home.

I left the tea shop determined to put the cottage on the market the very next day, and then get the hell away from that village and its murky secrets.

Instead of going back to the hotel, I

decided to walk down to the harbor. The idea of a strong sea breeze blowing the tangled cobwebs from my mind appealed to me far more than moping around in that dinky room.

The climb up the hill warmed my body against the chill of the wind, which now buffeted my face and tangled my hair. I reached the summit and looked down on the boats rocking on the water. Farther out, little white flecks of foam rode the top of the waves, and the sky above them had turned a dull gray.

The view from up there was so spectacular I wanted to enjoy it a while longer. An ancient-looking pub stood back from the road, with a bench in front of the window. I sat down and stretched my legs out to ease the ache of the climb.

From there I could see down the coast to a line of cliffs that disappeared into the mist. Dark clouds scudded across the sky, and the seagulls wheeled and swooped above the choppy waves. In no time at all goose bumps peppered my arms, and I considered going back to the hotel for a jacket. The reminder that if I wanted to see the harbor I'd have to climb back up the hill again dampened the idea.

I don't know why it didn't occur to me

that my journey down would do the same, but I started down, hoping that my burst of activity would warm up my blood again.

I was almost at the water's edge when without warning, the clouds opened up and a torrent of cold rain soaked my head and shoulders. I spotted a row of what appeared to be warehouses and hoping to find shelter, I hurried toward them.

There was no one about as I dashed across the concrete yard, but a door to one of the buildings stood slightly ajar and I slipped inside, shivering so hard my teeth rattled.

I seemed to be in a boatbuilder's warehouse. Right in front of me the skeleton of a boat loomed high above my head. A long bench lay behind it, covered in tools, mugs and a small TV set.

Rubbing my arms to get some feeling back into my hands, I stood just inside the door watching the rain splash into puddles. The warehouse smelled of sawdust and paint, and I hoped the rain would soon stop so I could get back into the fresh air.

Just as I was debating whether or not to brave getting wet, I heard deep male voices from somewhere in the back of the building. It occurred to me then that I was trespassing.

I started to leave, but one of the men caught sight of me and called out. I turned to explain, but the words fled from my mind when I saw Dan Connelly walking toward me.

"Hello, again," he said, as he approached. "Were you looking for me?"

"Actually I was taking shelter from the rain." Hot with embarrassment, I gestured out the door. "I was taking a walk to the harbor and got caught in it."

He seemed amused as his gaze swept over my hair, which I knew was hanging in dismal wet clumps around my face. "Better bring a jacket next time. Our English weather's unpredictable."

"Now you tell me." I rubbed my arms again. "I hope I didn't break any laws by coming in here."

"Don't worry, I'll bail you out if you end up in jail."

"Gee, thanks a lot."

"My pleasure." He opened the door wider and peered out at the spattering rain. "Come on, I'll give you a lift back to the hotel." Turning his head, he called out to someone behind him. "I'll get back to you with those figures, Jeff."

As a male voice answered him, I stepped outside, noticing for the first time the little red car parked at the end of the building. I was shivering again by the time we reached it and I was safely inside.

"So, how long will you be staying in Miles End?" Dan asked, as we drove out from the yard.

"I'm not sure. I guess it depends on how long it takes to sell the cottage."

"So you are selling it, then?"

I glanced at him, but he was staring straight ahead at the wet road. I wondered if he thought I might change my mind about selling now that I knew the truth about Gillian. It dawned on me then that there was more at stake than the sale of the cottage.

There was a family to consider — a family that might not be able to afford the rent a new owner would expect. What would happen to them if they had to move out?

I felt sick, knowing that I would be responsible for turning them out of their home. They weren't just any family. Even if I were related to them by marriage, they were the only relatives I had left in the world. How could I let them lose their home?

I sank back in the seat and answered Dan's question. "I don't know if I'm going to sell it. Quite honestly, I don't know what I'm going to do."

We reached the hotel a few minutes later.

"Don't mention it," Dan said, when I mumbled my thanks. "I'm usually buzzing around. If you need a lift somewhere, just call me."

"That's real kind of you," I began, "but —"

He silenced me with a raise of his hand. "No buts. I'm happy to oblige. I get tired of talking to myself when I'm driving. People are beginning to worry about me."

In spite of the turmoil going on in my mind, it surprised me how easy it was to smile at him. "Well, we can't have that. Thanks. I might take you up on the offer."

"Good." He waved at me and drove off.

I waited until he'd disappeared around the bend before heading up the steps. Now I had decisions to make. Gladys was right. I needed to talk to Gillian. It had to be face-to-face. The issues we had could not be resolved over the phone. In any case, there was no phone in my room. I had to use a public phone in the main hallway downstairs.

After drying my hair and putting on a dash of lipstick I went down to the public phone. An elderly woman had beaten me to it and judging by the way she was comfortably propped up against the wall, I figured she'd be there for a while.

I drifted down the hallway to take a look at the dining room, since I planned on eating there that evening. The passageway ended at a door with a glass window, through which I could see small, square tables covered in white tablecloths and a tiny vase of flowers on each one.

As I got closer and could view the entire room, I realized why the desk clerk had warned me to book for dinner. I counted eight tables in all, none of them big enough to accommodate more than four people, and squashed in at that. I thought about the pub on the hill. It probably offered meals, but a third climb back up to it was just too much for my legs to tackle, especially if the rain kept up.

I went back to the phone, just in time to hear the woman mutter, "She's coming back. I'd better go. You know how these Yanks are . . ." She hung up, sent me a furtive look and scurried away.

Wondering how she knew I was American and what she meant by that cryptic remark, I fished out Gillian's number from my pocket. She answered on the first ring.

I hadn't rehearsed what I was going to say, and I must have sounded stilted when I told her I would like to talk to her.

Her distant tone when she answered unnerved me. "What about?"

I didn't want to bring up the subject of her mother's involvement with Brandon. It sounded so callous on the phone. I'd planned to inch lightly into that dangerous territory one step at a time. Besides, if I told her the real reason for wanting a conversation with her she might very well refuse to see me. So I blurted out the first thing I could think of. "I think we should discuss what to do about the cottage."

"I thought you were going to sell it."

"Well, I am, but there are things we should discuss." I realized belatedly that it might have been better if I'd consulted a lawyer first and found out exactly what rights I had.

"All right." Gillian made no effort to hide her unwilling response. "When did you want to come?"

"Tomorrow?"

"You can come after dinner. About three o'clock."

I thought I'd misunderstood. "In the afternoon?"

"We have dinner at one on Sundays," Gillian said. "Old English custom."

I wasn't sure if she was being patronizing or not, and I had an uncomfortable feeling in my chest as I hung up. I knew this wasn't going to be easy. All I could hope was that I was up to the challenge.

CHAPTER 8

I decided to go back to the tea shop for dinner, rather than face a roomful of strangers all wary of "how Yanks are."

When I arrived at The Tea Parlor, however, I found it locked. Apparently Gladys closed early on a Saturday. In fact, all the shops on the main street were closed. The sidewalks were deserted, though a few cars still sped down the road at what I considered a reckless rate for such a narrow space.

Disappointed to be deprived of the Cornish pastie my mouth was already watering over, I wandered farther down the street and found a small restaurant open that vaguely resembled the fast-food places back home. I stared at the intriguing pictures of menu items on the wall, and considered the plate of fried chicken with a poached egg sitting on top. I played it safe and ordered chicken in a bun.

Jet lag had taken its toll again by the time

I arrived back at the hotel and I settled in for another early night. The next morning I braved the dining room and spent an uncomfortable breakfast being scrutinized by every eye in the room. Apparently word had gotten around that a Yank was staying at the hotel and no one was shy about displaying their curiosity.

I wondered if they were simply curious about a stranger in their midst, until I noticed the honeymoon couple I'd seen the day before smooching in the corner without so much as anyone glancing in their direction. It seemed that I was the center of attention — a position I really didn't want to occupy. I got out as quickly as I could.

It didn't occur to me until almost midday that I would need a ride to the cottage. The desk clerk, who told me his name was Ernie, assured me there was a taxi service, but since there was only one driver it might be unavailable. He obligingly called the number, then informed me that the taxi had been booked for the day. I'd have to find some other way to get there.

The bus service, Ernie also informed me, was erratic at best, and went in the wrong direction anyway. I considered calling Edward Perkins, but in the next second dismissed the idea. I didn't need him hover-

ing around while I had my chat with Gillian. It seemed as if I was in for a very long walk.

Then I thought of Dan. He had offered, after all, and much as I hated to take advantage of him so quickly, it would solve a problem if he could give me a ride.

I asked Ernie if he knew Dan, and wasn't really surprised when he told me Dan lived on his business premises. I felt nervous as I dialed, wondering if I'd taken his offer far too literally.

Dan's cheerful voice reassured me. "No, I'm not busy. I'll be right over."

"There's no rush," I assured him. "I don't have to be there until three."

"Good. That will give us time for a little sightseeing."

I hung up, feeling a little glow of pleasure at the prospect. Dan was good company, and right then I couldn't think of anything I'd enjoy more than having him show me the sights.

He arrived a few minutes later. I was determined to put my meeting with Gillian out of my mind for the next hour and just enjoy the ride.

Cairnmouth Castle, it turned out, was farther down the coast, and took twenty minutes to reach. I saw its gray walls and

square turrets sitting on top of a hill long before we reached it. A few people straggled up the steep road, and I was thankful for my comfortable seat as we sailed past them.

"It gets pretty crowded in the summer," Dan explained as he pulled into a small grassy parking lot. "Tourists come in from Stattenham and Chatswell — they're our two closest towns. The season's just about over now, though. This place will be deserted in another month."

"It's beautiful." I stared in awe at the magnificent towering walls with their tiny slit windows. "This is how it must have looked hundreds of years ago, when real knights in armor rode across the drawbridge and ladies in flowing silk gowns rushed out to meet them."

"And backed off again when they realized that knights in battle don't bathe for months on end. Can you imagine how they must have stunk?"

I gave him a mock frown. "Obviously you're not a romantic."

He grinned. "A realist, that's me. Sorry if I spoiled your fantasy."

"Nothing you say could spoil this." I looked back at the castle and tried to imagine English royalty strolling through what must have once been the rose gardens,

or gazing at the water spouting from the now-dry ornamental fountains.

Above the spacious grounds white clouds chased one another across a deep blue sky, and seagulls soared across the castle turrets, looking for scraps dropped by the tourists. Watching two young children hang over one of the walls, a warm sense of peace crept over me.

I let out my breath on a sigh of pure rapture. "This is history," I murmured. "I've never seen anything so ancient, or so inspiring."

Dan's voice brought me out of my trance. "You really are impressed by all this, aren't you."

I smiled at him. "I really am."

"Want to go inside for a closer look?"

"Oh, I'd love to!" I turned eagerly toward him, then remembered where I had to be that afternoon. "I really don't have time, though," I added with real regret. "I told Gillian I'd be there at three, and I don't want to be late."

His curiosity showed in his face when he looked at me. "You've come to a decision then."

I wondered why he was so interested in my plans for the cottage and wanted to ask if he was thinking of buying it, then thought better of it. I didn't want to discuss the sale of the cottage with him or anyone else. I still couldn't make up my mind what to do about it, and I was beginning to dread my visit with Gillian.

"Not yet," I said lightly. "There's a lot to consider."

He put the car into reverse and backed out of the parking spot before answering me. "Well, if you're going to be around for a little while, I could show you the inside of the castle before you go back."

I made an effort to tone down my excitement. "I'd enjoy that. I've never seen the inside of a castle."

"Then it's a date."

I watched his hands turn the wheel. They looked strong, tanned almost bronze, like his face. He must have spent a lot of time out in the sun. "I think I should rent a car," I said, as the idea popped into my mind. "Is there someone around here I can rent from?"

"Not in Miles End. You'd have to go to town for one." He sent me a quick glance, his eyes squinting against the sunlight. "You're planning on staying around for a while, then?"

"For a while, yes."

I couldn't tell if he was pleased about that

or not, and it unsettled me that it mattered.

"I can take you into town to find a car rental," Dan said, as we sped up the coast road.

I still wasn't comfortable riding on the wrong side of the road, and I put my little quiver of nerves down to that. "I've already taken up enough of your time," I said carefully. "I can probably get a bus into the town, can't I?"

"You could, but it will be a lot faster and a heck of a lot more comfortable by car." He slowed to a crawl as we approached the main street of Miles End. "Besides, I have to go into Stattenham tomorrow, anyway. I'd enjoy the company."

"Thank you. I'd really appreciate that." I smiled at him and he gave me a brief smile back before turning to watch the road.

Before I was really prepared we arrived at the cottage.

"I'll hang around if you like? Give you a lift back?"

Regretfully I shook my head. I'd imposed enough. "Thanks, but the walk back will do me good."

"See you tomorrow then. Pick you up at three?"

"Sounds good. Thanks." I climbed out of the car, wishing I had the nerve to ask him to come in with me. His moral support would have been reassuring.

Much as I wanted to know everything I could about Brandon's affair with Eileen, I knew it was bound to be awkward discussing it with Gillian. I could only hope she would be at least halfway willing to tell me what she knew.

I watched Dan drive off and felt a moment's panic, before I reminded myself that I'd come three thousand miles to get answers, and the only way I was going to get them was to deal with Gillian as best I could.

She answered the door, and I was struck by the change in her. Her light brown hair now curled softly against her cheeks, and she'd made up her eyes. Her clear skin glowed, and the pale lavender dress she wore gave her an air of sophistication. She looked quite pretty.

My gaze dropped instinctively to her feet. They were snuggled in a pair of black shoes with enough heel to make her a good head taller than me. Gillian, I realized, was dressed for battle.

If she'd hoped to intimidate me, I silently vowed, she was in for a surprise. Though I'd have felt a good deal more comfortable if I'd consulted that lawyer and was sure of my rights.

I followed her into the tiny living room, trying to convince myself that she'd dressed that way for church and just hadn't bothered to change. The appetizing smell of cooking made me realize I'd skipped lunch. I tried not to notice my stomach growling as I sat down on the same chair I'd occupied the day before.

"Would you like a cup of tea?" Gillian asked, hovering in the entrance to the hallway.

"Thank you, no." I didn't want to waste any more time than necessary.

"Well, did you want to see over the house, then?"

"In a little while." I hesitated, then added, "I'd like to talk to you first."

She pinched her lips in the way I'd seen Brandon do so many times. "Look, if you're going to sell my house then there's not much I can do about it, is there. But I tell you right now, none of us are happy about it. This is our home, and my children are miserable that they have to leave."

"I'm sure they are. But —"

"I don't know what we're going to do, I really don't. It's not easy to find another place we could afford in Miles End, and it would cost even more to live in one of the towns. Ned would have to drive all the way back and forth every day. These roads are murder in the winter, and in the summer they're crowded with visitors — it would take him hours longer to get home."

Feeling at a disadvantage, I stood up again. "I understand how you feel, but —"

Gillian took a step toward me. "Do you, Mrs. Maitland? I don't think you do. My father bought this house for my mother and me, and I honestly don't understand how *you* ended up with it."

Frankly, I didn't understand, either. Surely Brandon must have known how much trouble his decision would cause for both Gillian and me. The truth was, I really did understand how she felt. But I wanted her to know how I felt, too. It was bad enough my husband had kept his daughter a secret from me, but to be treated like the guilty party in all this was infuriating. It was time I stated my case and this time I intended to stand my ground.

"Brandon must have had his reasons to leave me the cottage," I said evenly. "It was obviously what he wanted. He may have bought the cottage for you and your mother, but it was still his to do with as he wished."

Gillian's eyes burned with resentment as

she stared at me across that quiet room. "It was all your fault," she said, her voice low with contained anger. "If he hadn't met you he'd have married my mother and we'd have been living in America, instead of stuck in this crummy little town all our lives."

"You can't blame that on me. I didn't even know your mother existed until a few months ago."

"But you did take him away from her. She died of a broken heart, you know. She never got over him. She still loved him, even after he walked out on us and left us to starve. It's all right for you. You don't know what it was like growing up without a father. Not having any money for nice clothes or Christmas presents or going on holiday like the rest of the kids."

"Yes," I said quietly, "as a matter of fact, I do. I know exactly how it feels. And I'm sorry you had such a miserable time. I really am. But I refuse to accept the blame for something I had no control over. Brandon never told me about you and your mother." Suddenly remembering something, I added, "But you knew that. You told Gladys you were worried about me finding out about you."

Gillian shrugged. "So I knew. It doesn't change anything."

I wrinkled my brow at her. "So how did you know?"

She lowered her eyes and turned away from me. "I wrote to him, didn't I. When my mother died. I got his address from the county office where he paid the taxes on the house. I thought he'd want to know."

And I'd had no idea. It must have been hard for him to keep something so heart wrenching from me. Then again, Brandon was an expert at hiding things. "He wrote back to you?"

"Yeah." Her laugh was anything but amusing. "The only letter I ever got from him. You know what he said?" She edged closer to an armchair and smoothed her hands along the back of it as if drawing comfort from the gesture. "He said he was sorry, but he had another life now and he didn't want me to write again. He said there was no sense in hurting you now, when it was so long ago."

She looked up, and the anger that had sustained me until then collapsed when I saw tears in her eyes. "He never cared how much he was hurting me, though, did he?"

I wanted to go to her, to put an arm around those proud shoulders and cry with her, for all of us. I just couldn't make myself move. "I'm sorry," I said, hoping I could put enough into those simple words to convince her I meant it.

I wondered if Gillian had sent the picture to Brandon. I wanted to ask her, but just then a door slammed, shattering the moment.

Gillian jumped back from the chair and dashed a hand across her eyes. "Ned? Is that you?"

A gruff voice answered her from down the hallway.

"Come here," Gillian called back. "Mrs. Maitland's here."

Footsteps trudged down the hallway and a tall, rangy man with a shock of red hair stepped into the room. His attention flicked over me, then he looked at his wife.

"Meet Mrs. Maitland," Gillian said.

Ned Hodge turned to me and touched his forehead in a disarming old-fashioned salute. "Afternoon, m'm."

"I'm pleased to meet you," I said awkwardly.

He nodded, and sent another look at his wife as if asking for approval.

"Where are the kids?" Gillian demanded.

"Out the back." Ned nudged his head at the hallway.

"Well, tell them to come in. I want them to meet Mrs. Maitland."

He looked worried. "They're none too clean. They've been climbing up the big oak."

Gillian's frown deepened. "In their best clothes? I told 'em not to get their clothes dirty. Why didn't you watch them? Fetch them kids in here this minute."

Without a word Ned tramped off down the hallway, and a moment later the door slammed once more.

"Bloody kids," Gillian muttered. "They never do what they're told."

"Maybe I should go," I said, moving toward the door.

"No, wait."

Gillian moved deeper into the room, and I saw that her mascara had smudged. That small sign of vulnerability tugged at me. Whether she liked it or not, we had something in common. We'd both survived a bitter childhood without a father, and if my guess was right, with a mother who'd buried herself in the past.

"I'd like you to meet the children," Gillian said. "They're good kids. They shouldn't have to be uprooted from their home."

So she was playing on my sympathy, hoping I'd feel guilty about throwing her kids out on the street. I couldn't blame her. I'd do the same if I were fighting for my kids. Except I'd never had kids. Brandon had seen to that.

It occurred to me then to wonder how I hadn't gotten pregnant. Brandon had never used protection. He must have had a vasectomy or something. And lied about it. Once more the questions were pounding in my brain, but it was too late to find the answers now. The kids had arrived.

They'd tumbled down the hallway and spilled into the living room in a rush of boundless energy. There were only three of them, but in those cramped quarters it felt like a dozen.

I recognized Robbie, the little boy I'd met yesterday. The other two looked to be close in age, though the boy was inches taller than the girl. "Hi," I said, as three pairs of eyes studied me with frank curiosity. "I'm Marjorie." I smiled at the little boy. "Hello, Robbie. We've already met, haven't we."

Robbie nodded, one thumb going to his mouth.

The little girl gave his hand a light tap. "Don't suck your thumb." She turned back to me. "My name's Sheila," she announced. "An' he's Craig." She pointed at her brother. "He's older than me, but only a year. I'm two years older than Robbie." She held up two fingers for emphasis.

Craig had the same blue eyes and red hair as his father, but Sheila was a Maitland through and through, with brown pigtails halfway down her back. She looked up at me with Brandon's smile, and my heart melted.

"This is Mrs. Maitland," Gillian said, and started to say something else, but Craig interrupted her.

"I know who she is," he said, with a scowl in my direction. "She's the lady that's going to take our house away from us."

I hurried to reassure him. "No, Craig, I'm not going to take the house away." I looked at Gillian, who refused to meet my eyes. "There's no need for you to move out. I'm sure the new owner will be nice about it, and you can all stay here."

Gillian uttered a dry laugh. "Do you know how much rent they can charge for a place like this?"

I was about to answer when I felt a small hand creep into mine. I looked down into Robbie's little face, and my arms ached to hold him.

" 'Lo Grandma," he said. "Can we come and live with you?"

"Don't be silly, Robbie," Craig said, pulling him out of my grasp. "She's not

Grandma. Grandma's gone to heaven, isn't she. Mummy says she's with Grandpa now."

The room seemed to have become uncomfortably warm. I stared at Gillian, but she kept her attention firmly on her children. I don't know how I managed it, but my voice sounded perfectly calm when I spoke. "I really must go, now." I said goodbye to all three children, but only Robbie answered me.

Somehow I got out the door and down the path without stumbling. Jet lag, I told myself. I needed to eat something.

It wasn't until I was on the road that I realized I had a very long walk ahead of me. To make matters worse, tears spilled down my face and no matter how hard I dabbed at them with a crumpled tissue, more fell to take their place.

I really didn't know why I cried. I thought I'd finished shedding tears over Brandon and the wasted years. It seemed I was wrong.

CHAPTER 9

I took huge gulps of air, blinked hard and blew my nose.

Just then a horn tooted behind me. Although there was no sidewalk, I was walking along the grass verge, well out of the way of traffic. Irritated, I turned my head to scowl at the impatient driver.

Dan grinned back at me from behind the wheel of his little red car. Hoping I hadn't made too much mess of my face, I waited for him to pull up beside me.

"I thought I'd hang around anyway," he said, when he opened the passenger door. "Just in case you changed your mind about the lift."

Grateful for his insight, I scrambled in, avoiding his gaze. "You should be charging fares," I said, as I settled down on the seat.

To my relief, he acted as if he hadn't noticed my tearstained cheeks. "Well, as a matter of fact, I was thinking of assessing payment."

He'd sounded perfectly serious, and I didn't want to look at him to check if he was smiling. "I'll be happy to buy gas," I offered. "I hear it's very expensive over here."

"Hideously expensive. But that wasn't what I had in mind."

I ventured a glance at him and noticed a dimple flash in his cheek. "I'd offer my firstborn, except I don't have any."

He looked at me then, and I saw sympathy in his eyes. "Nothing that drastic." He turned back to the road. "As long as we're going into town tomorrow to find you a car, I thought it might be nice if you joined me for dinner. I know where there's a quiet little restaurant that serves good food and wine. Not a patch on Glad's pasties, of course, but good for second best."

Taken by surprise, I tried not to sound like a breathless schoolgirl. "As long as you don't tell Gladys we went. I don't want her feeling we've been disloyal."

He lifted his hand and drew the back of his thumb across his mouth. "Zipped. I swear."

"In that case, I accept." I settled back, enjoying the warmth creeping back into my body. "On one condition."

"Uh-oh. I should have known there'd be a catch."

"No catch. I just want to go dutch."

"Not on your life. When I take a lady out, I pay."

I liked that. "All right, I won't argue. Thank you."

We sat in companionable silence for a while and had almost reached the hotel before Dan spoke again. "I'll see you around three, then."

I'd been frantically wondering what I could find to wear for our dinner date. I hadn't brought anything dressy with me, mostly pants and tops. On my trips down the main street I hadn't seen any place, other than a maternity shop, that sold clothes, and I wasn't about to accentuate my less-than-trim waistline.

"I'll be ready," I said, as I scrambled out of the car. "I'm looking forward to it."

His eyes crinkled at the edges as he grinned at me. "Me, too."

I watched him drive away, wondering what I would have done if he hadn't appointed himself my benefactor.

There was a message waiting for me when I got back to my room. Apparently Val had called, and asked that I call her back. I felt guilty, knowing I should have let her know

I'd arrived safely. I just hadn't felt like talking to her where anyone passing by could hear my conversation. I really needed to look into cell-phone service.

I went back down to the main hallway and put a call through to the club. The woman who answered told me Val was at home, which surprised me. Val was hardly ever at home, even on weekends. She spent most of her waking hours at the club.

I got through to her at her condo, and was upset to hear she'd sprained an ankle. "I fell off a treadmill," she said, her voice, thick with disgust, echoing across six thousand miles of telephone wire with surprising clarity. "Can you freakin' believe that?"

I could, and the vision made me wince. "I'm sorry," I said. "You must be going out of your mind with boredom."

"Not really. I've got good company."

I knew by the way she said it that she meant a man. For some reason I thought of Dan, and how comfortable he was to be with.

"So tell me, did you meet her?"

"No, not exactly." I peered up and down the hallway. Although it was empty for the moment, I knew Ernie was hovering behind the counter and could probably hear every word I said.

Val, of course, was not about to let it go at that. "So, what happened?"

I lowered my voice. "She's dead."

"She's what?" Val's voice rose to a shriek. "No way! What happened? You didn't kill her, did you?"

"Of course not. She died a few years ago." I realized I didn't know exactly how long ago. That was something else I'd like to find out.

"So the cottage is empty? That's a bit of luck. You'll be able to sell it without any problems."

"Well, no, I can't." Footsteps sounded in the hallway and a middle-aged couple nodded at me as they passed by on their way to the dining room. I glanced at my watch. Of course, it was close to dinnertime. Apparently not everyone in England ate their Sunday dinner at midday. "Val, I'm sorry, I can't talk now. I just wanted to let you know I'm fine and everything is going well."

"It doesn't sound like it." Val sounded grumpy.

"No, really, everything's fine. I'll call you again when I can talk, all right?" I hung up, feeling even more guilty. Val had obviously been looking forward to hearing all the juicy gossip, and I'd cut her off without telling her anything.

The truth was, I didn't feel like telling her. This whole situation was so personal, still so painful for both Gillian and me, I'd feel disloyal discussing it all with someone who was too far removed from any of it to truly understand.

I consoled myself with the thought that I couldn't discuss anything as long as there were people within earshot. If I wanted any kind of conversation with Val, I'd have to find some other way to communicate with her.

Right now, though, my growling stomach reminded me it had been some time since I'd eaten. I assumed the tea shop was closed, and I really didn't relish the idea of another fast-food meal. The only other option open to me meant a hard climb up to the pub, unless I squeezed myself into the dining room.

I wondered if Dan was eating dinner alone. I missed his company, and that worried me — I didn't want to rely on him.

Only now was I beginning to realize how much control Brandon had had over my life. Never again would I let a man rule me that way. With that vow firmly fixed in my mind, I went to look for an empty seat in the dining room.

A few minutes later I found myself

crammed between a lady with a nasty case of sunburn and her frail-looking husband, who sat through the whole meal without saying a word. Not that he'd have much chance since his wife didn't stop talking.

I bolted down my fish and chips and escaped to my room as soon as I could manage it. The weariness that had attacked me the previous two evenings seemed less oppressive, so I sat down and wrote a long letter to Val on the hotel stationery.

I started by describing the village, then told her about Gillian. I'd never told Val why I didn't have children, so I left out the bit about Brandon's lie. That was still too painful to mention. I ended up writing about my trip to the castle. I mentioned Dan only as my driver, but I knew Val would pick up on it, and would want to know everything about him, right up to what kind of aftershave he wore.

I laid down the pen, smiling at the thought. I liked his aftershave. It was appealing without being overpowering. Which pretty much described his personality. After deciding I was giving entirely too much thought to Dan Connelly, I switched on the television, thankful for at least one modern amenity.

Edward Perkins called the next day, wanting to know when I intended to put the cottage up for sale. Once more I was faced with calling him back from my very public telephone, or actually going to see him.

I decided to visit Gladys first. I wanted to sip a cup of coffee at a table where I could raise my elbow without fear of poking someone in the eye.

Gladys greeted me like a long-lost friend, linking her arm through mine as she led me to a window table. "Dan told me you went to see Gillian yesterday," she said, as I sat down. "He stopped by here this morning on his way down to the barber."

I wondered if he was getting a haircut for our date that night, then realized how absurd I was being. He was simply being nice to an out-of-town visitor, and I was making entirely too much of the whole thing.

"Yes," I said, answering Gladys's comment. "I met her husband and the other two children."

"Ah, that Ned is a quiet one, I tell you. Never has much to say. Nor do for that matter. He's a bit old-fashioned that way. It's Gillian that does everything. Takes care of the kiddies and the house, as well as works at the school cafeteria all week. Now that Robbie's at school all day with the other kiddies it's a bit easier on her, though."

She went off to get me some coffee and Danish, and I studied the menu in an effort to stop worrying about my dinner date and what I was going to wear.

A few minutes later she returned with my order. "Janice didn't turn up again this morning," she said, squeezing herself onto the chair opposite me. "Good job we're not busy."

That was an understatement, considering I was the only customer in the room. I thought uneasily that this would give Gladys a good opportunity to ask awkward questions. I was right.

"So how'd you like being a grandmother to three kiddies, then?" she asked, as I tackled the large pastry she'd brought me.

"I'm not really their grandmother."

"Stepgrandmother, then. To those kiddies it's the same thing."

"Not to Gillian, though." I stopped eating and reluctantly added, "The children are adorable, of course. I'd like nothing better than to claim them as my grandchildren, but I can tell you right now, Gillian is not going to bend."

Gladys looked sympathetic. "Gave you a hard time, did she?"

"You could say that." I wondered how

much I should tell her, then decided not to say any more.

"Still blames you for taking her father away, does she?"

I nodded. "This pastry is really good."

My attempt at changing the conversation had no effect on Gladys's determination to learn all there was to know. "She'll come around, like I told you. It'll just take time, that's all."

"Well, time is something I haven't got." I picked up my napkin and dabbed at my mouth. "I have to get back home and take care of some urgent matters over there. Like finding a place to live for one, and getting a job."

Gladys seemed upset by that. "I thought you were going to stay a while. Get to know the Hodges."

"No." I reached for my coffee. "There's no point. I'm going to put the cottage up for sale, find a lawyer to handle things and then I'm going home." Right then that seemed the most comforting decision I'd made in a long time.

"So you're giving up. Running away, is that it?"

There was enough disgust in her voice to offend me. "I wouldn't call it that," I said carefully. "I'm doing the most sensible thing for all of us. Gillian obviously resents me, so I'm getting out of her hair."

"Out of her life, you mean."

It was on the tip of my tongue to tell Gladys she was meddling too much, however well she meant it. Before I could say anything, though, she reached out and patted my hand.

"I just don't want to see you do something you'll regret," she said. "I know it's none of my business, and I'm talking out of turn, but you have no idea how much Gillian and those kids need you. That girl is so miserable, and she's making everyone around her miserable, too. She misses her mum, and she's fed up with her life, and I'm afraid she'll do something really silly if someone isn't there to keep an eye on her."

A stab of anxiety made me look up. "What do you mean?"

Gladys smoothed back a strand of gray hair with her stubby fingers. "Well, you know, something that might hurt them all."

"You mean leave her husband?"

"The kiddies, too. Or maybe worse, like doing herself some harm." Gladys shook her head. "I'm not saying she'd do anything that drastic, mind, but I know by some of the things she's told me that it's crossed her mind."

I felt sick as I set my coffee cup back in its saucer. "She seems so strong. I can't imagine her leaving her family to fend for themselves."

"It takes a strong person to do that."

She was right about that. I'd often thought about leaving Brandon. I just hadn't had the strength to do it. "Well, I'm sure she's just depressed. I know how that can make you feel. I've been through it myself."

"I bet you have." Gladys put both hands on the table and heaved herself to her feet. "Just remember this. The Hodges are the closest thing to a family you have now. Do you really want to turn your back on them? Something that's really good never comes easy, does it. It just might be worth you hanging around for a little while and see if you two can't work things out together." The doorbell jangled just then, and she left me to greet the new arrivals.

I finished my pastry and coffee, then left a couple of bills on the table to cover the breakfast and a tip. Gladys waved to me as I went out, and I smiled back, even though I didn't feel like smiling. What she'd told me deeply disturbed me, and I had much to think about before I went to see Perkins.

I stopped by the post office to mail my letter, and the morning air had warmed considerably by the time I got back to the hotel. Up in my room, I opened the window and leaned out. The dark blue ocean seemed as still as a carpet, and the sky above it was empty of clouds. I wondered how many more lovely days I'd see like this before I left this charming little town. October was less than a week away.

I thought about the relentless dark skies back home and the constant rain that drenched the city for so much of the winter and early spring. The thought of hunting for a place to live depressed me.

The idea of living somewhere like Miles End intrigued me. Its antiquated streets and lack of the modern conveniences I'd taken for granted back home would present quite a challenge.

I thought about Gillian's comment. *Stuck in this crummy little town all our lives.* Had she really been thinking of deserting her family, I wondered, or was that just Gladys's way of persuading me to stay a while?

I had to admit, the idea had its benefits. I enjoyed the peace and quiet — such a contrast to the noise and chaos of rush hour on the bustling streets of downtown Seattle.

What else had Gladys said? *Something that's really good never comes easy, does it.* She was right. I'd longed to have a real family, and yet I was turning my back on the closest I'd ever come to having one. Not only that, if I left now I'd never have the answers I wanted so badly.

If Gillian and I could find some way to communicate, maybe we could find the answers together. We both needed to understand why Brandon had done what he did. The answers were buried somewhere in the past, and only by sharing what we knew could we unearth them.

I pulled my head back into the room and paced back and forth, arguing with myself. There were a dozen reasons why I should fly back to Seattle and let a lawyer handle the sale. I needed a place to live, and a job. My home was there, people I knew, a life I was accustomed to living.

Here everyone was a stranger, and the lifestyle and culture were so alien to me I might as well be on another planet. Yet there was a bond here that could never be fulfilled if I left.

Here was the last connection to a man to whom I'd given close to thirty years, a man I'd never really understood. Here was the chance to have the daughter I'd yearned for, and the grandkids my arms had longed to hold. Here was family, and that was something I could never find back in Seattle.

The task ahead of me was formidable. Gillian was a fortress I'd have to breach, and I was not very good at taking on a battle. I would much rather turn the other cheek and walk away.

Something that's really good never comes easy.

What I needed was a place to start, I decided. A common ground between Gillian and me. I halted in the middle of the room. I knew what I had to do. And I knew where to start. The complications were awesome. I didn't even know if I could make it work, but I was willing to give it a shot.

Tomorrow, I told myself. By then I'd have a car at my disposal. Tomorrow I would put phase one of my plan into action. It was amazing how much better that made me feel.

In anticipation of my dinner that night I skipped lunch, making do with a candy bar I bought from Ernie. I wasted an hour trying on everything in my limited wardrobe, and rejecting everything the second I put it on. I wondered if I'd have time to shop in Stattenham, assuming there were clothes stores there.

I soon dismissed that idea. I didn't want Dan thinking I was putting too much importance on our date. In fact, I had better stop thinking of it as a date, I warned myself. We would be in town together and sharing a meal. That was all.

I couldn't imagine why I was being so jittery over such a casual acquaintance. I was quite sure he'd be horrified if he knew. Besides that, I felt guilty, though there was no reason on earth why I should.

True, my husband had been dead only four months, but my relationship with Dan was perfectly innocent. My silliness over the whole thing was just a result of being thousands of miles away from home and all the upheaval I'd been through.

I felt as though I were living a different life, and I no longer wanted to go back to the old one. I felt energized, more confident than I ever remembered being, and if that security was destined to be shaken now and again, I felt more positive about handling things. Eventually.

Dan arrived a few minutes early and was waiting for me when I went down to the foyer. I saw him lounging against the counter, chatting with Ernie, who caught sight of me as I came down the stairs and sent me a knowing wink that unsettled me. I could imagine the gossip that would be winging through the grapevine.

Dan straightened when he saw me and

lifted his hand in a salute. I'd decided on a pair of black pants that were supposed to have a slimming effect, and a pale blue linen shirt that I hoped was dressy enough for the occasion. Just in case the weather turned on me again, I'd draped a black cardigan over my arm.

I was relieved to see Dan wearing casual slacks and a polo shirt under his jacket. I wasn't too underdressed after all. I joined him in front of the counter, aware of Ernie's focus on us.

"All set?" Dan asked, and I nodded.

I glanced at Ernie, who watched us the way a kid watches someone serve up ice cream. "Dan was kind enough to offer a ride into Stattenham," I told him. "I need to rent a car." Mad at myself for feeling it necessary to explain where we were going, I headed for the main door. I had almost reached it when Ernie called out after us, "Enjoy your dinner, you two."

I raised my eyebrows at Dan as he opened the door for me.

He gave me his appealing grin. "Ernie asked me if I planned to have dinner here tonight, so I told him we were having dinner in Stattenham. Hope you don't mind."

"Of course I don't mind." It seemed that if I was going to stick around for a while,

I'd better get used to everyone knowing my business. I wondered what Gladys would say when she heard the news. Then I put it out of my mind. I was looking forward to the evening out, and I was going to enjoy it.

CHAPTER 10

The town of Stattenham was bigger than I expected, though it had the old-world air about it that had enchanted me in Miles End. Some of the buildings were fairly modern, but most had withstood centuries of abuse from the weather, exhaust fumes and the passing of time, not to mention bombing during the Second World War.

Dan, as usual, enthralled me with all kinds of historical facts and figures as we drove through the busy streets. I hung on to his every word, fascinated by the glimpses of a world so alien to mine.

We spent some time deciding on a car rental. I finally picked a Toyota, since I was familiar with the car, though I felt disoriented when I sat behind the wheel.

"This is going to take some getting used to," I told Dan, as he opened the door for me to climb out again. "I don't know if I can drive on the wrong side of the road."

"Then don't drive on the wrong side. The left side is the right side. Remember that and you can't go wrong."

I made a face at him. "Thanks for your help."

He grinned back at me. "Just remember to keep the passenger seat between you and the curb. It might get tricky going around corners for a bit, so watch the traffic and avoid the roundabouts like the plague. They can really mess you up."

"Roundabouts?"

He drew a circle in the air with his hand. "Those little round islands with all the roads branching off it. Even I get confused on those sometimes."

"You're not exactly making my day."

"Don't worry." He put a friendly arm around my shoulders. "You can follow me back to your hotel. As long as you stay close behind me, you'll be okay."

Comforted by his words, I tried not to let the weight of his arm unsettle me as he steered me back to his car. We'd made arrangements to pick up the rental after we'd had dinner, and we spent the next hour or two exploring the town.

I was enchanted by the narrow streets and steep hills, and kept stopping to peer into shop windows. A display of Toby mugs caught my eye. The decorative mugs, all fashioned into different faces, made me smile. "I've seen pictures of mugs like these," I told Dan, "but I've never seen a real one. Do you mind if we go in to look at them?"

"Your wish is my command, fair damsel." He opened the door for me, setting off a jangling bell that reminded me of The Tea Parlor in Miles End.

I resisted the urge to curtsy and stepped inside the shop.

Shelves upon shelves of treasures stretched out before me, and eagerly I rushed to explore. Exquisite cut-glass castles, delicate bone-china ladies dressed in period costumes, china rabbits dressed like the characters in Beatrix Potter books, all begged to be taken home.

It was just as well, I reflected, that I had to watch my spending, or I'd have to buy another suitcase just to take all the souvenirs back home with me. Eventually, and with great reluctance, I headed for the door, where Dan stood waiting for me. With a last look around that bewitching shop, I stepped out into the street.

"Getting hungry?"

I nodded at Dan's question. "Starving."

"Good. The restaurant is a few minutes

away." He took my arm in that proprietary gesture of his, and walked me back to the car.

The Cove was more than a good restaurant. Or maybe the company I was in made everything seem so magical. From the soft glow of the pink lamps around the walls, the burgundy tablecloths and pink roses on the tables, to the dreamy piano music and excellent French wine, I couldn't have dreamed up a more romantic atmosphere.

I ordered Dover sole, after Dan told me that I'd be getting the real thing. He was right. It was delicious.

He asked questions about Seattle, and I answered as best I could, avoiding anything about my personal life. I wasn't sure how much he knew, and I didn't want to share the gory details with him.

After enjoying a cup of extra-strong coffee, I asked him the question that had been nudging me ever since I'd met him. "Did you know Eileen Robbins?"

He took his time answering, stirring sugar into his coffee until I was sure he'd put a hole in the bottom of the cup. "Yes," he said at last. "I knew her."

I felt a strange little pang of resentment, though I couldn't imagine why. "What was she like?"

I didn't know I was going to ask him that, but now that I'd posed the question, I couldn't wait to hear the answer.

His expression was hard to gauge when he looked up. "Quiet little thing," he said, surprising me. "Didn't have much to say, kept to herself. She didn't seem to have too many friends. Nothing like Gillian. That girl must take after her father." His face changed, as if he'd realized he'd said something that might upset me.

I knew then, that he did know the whole story. "It's all right," I told him. "I've gotten over the shock of finding out I have a stepdaughter. I'm even getting used to the fact that everyone in Miles End knows my business."

"Not everyone." His smile was wary. "There are a few farmers on the outskirts of town who might still be in the dark."

His attempt at humor eased my tense fingers and I put down my cup. "Well, that's a relief."

"I'm sorry, Marjorie." He seemed about to reach for my hand then apparently changed his mind. "I can only imagine how tough this is for you."

"It hasn't been easy. I suppose in everyone's mind I'm the villain of the piece. Gillian's convinced I took her father away from her and her mother, even though I knew nothing about them."

Sympathy clouded his eyes. "Miles End is a small town. People hang together, protect their own. You're the stranger, the outsider. That's all. Once they get to know you and find out what a nice lady you are, they'll accept that there are two sides to the story."

"I really don't care about other people." I felt my throat constrict and switched my gaze to a painting of a lighthouse on the wall. "I just care about Gillian and her family. I want to make peace with her, try to make her understand."

"You know, you remind me a little bit of Eileen."

Shocked, I stared at him. "In what way?"

"You seem to have this hidden core of strength that you don't want anyone to know about. Sort of tough on the inside, soft on the outside. It's an interesting combination."

"Thank you. I think."

His smile seemed to warm my whole body. "I meant it in the nicest possible way."

The conversation was getting a little too personal for comfort. I changed it by asking him about his business, and then listened in fascination as he described what seemed to me an astonishing assortment of items that he stored in his warehouse. Engine parts, sports and fishing equipment — the list went on and on. I couldn't imagine how he kept track of everything.

I was about to ask him that when he dismayed me by saying, "I'm thinking of giving it up, though. I can't compete any more with the big boys, and most people come into town here to pick up their supplies at the discount stores. They're squeezing us little guys out one by one."

"What will you do if you give it up?"

He shrugged. "Get a job in one of the towns, I suppose. I'm a pretty good carpenter. I'll find work."

"It will be tough working for someone else when you've been your own boss for so long."

"A lot less stress, though. I'm getting tired of working day and night, week after week. It's time I had a little fun before I get too old to get out of an armchair."

I smiled. "You have a long way to go before that happens."

"And I intend to make the most of it."

Our waiter arrived just then with the bill, putting an end to what was once again drifting into a personal conversation. It had been a pleasurable evening, and I left the restaurant thinking that the memory of it would stay with me.

The trip back to Miles End was something else. Once we left the town, the dark country roads seemed to swallow me up in shadows, and every time I watched Dan's taillights disappear around a bend I felt sure I would end up in a field.

By the time we drew up outside The White Stone Inn my knees shook. Dan was waiting for me as I climbed out of the Toyota, and his cheerful voice echoed across the empty street.

"There, that wasn't so bad, was it?"

"Scared me to death," I told him, as I locked the car door. I slipped the keys into my pants pocket. "If I hadn't been following you I'd be sleeping with the cows tonight in some farmer's field."

His laugh rang out, soothing my jangled nerves. "Well, you can always get a lift with me if you get too nervous to drive. I'm going to miss your company."

I felt a stab of misgiving. I'd no longer have an excuse to call him. I'd miss him, too, I realized. More than I should.

As if reading my mind, he moved a little closer. "Don't forget we have a date to explore the castle. Just let me know when you can go and I'll try to get away."

"I can go anytime," I said, afraid that if I

didn't arrange the trip we might not get to go.

"Okay. Let's say day after tomorrow, about eleven? Will that work for you? We can have lunch afterward."

"Perfect." That would give me time to get things settled with Gillian, I thought, and then I could relax and look forward to our date. "But this time I'm paying."

"What is it with you women? Always worrying about who's paying. I asked, I pay. All right?"

"No," I said firmly. "It's not all right. I can't keep accepting your hospitality without returning it. It's un-American."

His teeth gleamed white in the darkness. "Un-American, huh? Well, I tell you what. You can come over my place and cook dinner for me one night. How's that?"

My rush of pleasure made my voice husky. "That I can do. As long as I get to pick the menu."

He gave me an old-fashioned bow with a sweeping gesture of his hand. "I accept with pleasure, fair lady."

This time I did curtsy. I was still smiling as I hurried up the steps to the hotel.

I slept soundly that night and awoke to the plaintive cries of the seagulls outside my window. Looking out, I saw gray skies and rain sweeping across the street. Thank heavens I had a car and wouldn't have to walk to Perkins's office.

I called him from the foyer and made an appointment to see him later that morning. Then I went down to The Tea Parlor for coffee and Danish.

Gladys sat down with me as usual, and immediately asked me how I'd enjoyed my dinner with Dan the night before.

I couldn't believe I actually felt guilty. "How did you know?"

"Ernie. He said he saw you two leaving the hotel."

"I needed to rent a car and Dan was kind enough to offer me a ride into Stattenham."

Gladys nodded. "I saw you park it outside." She tilted her head to one side. "Getting friendly, you two, aren't you?"

Irritated to feel my cheeks warming, I muttered, "Dan's been very helpful. I don't know how I would have gotten around if he hadn't been there to offer me a ride."

"Dan's like that. Always holding out a helping hand. Does it for everyone, he does."

Okay, I got it. She was warning me not to take Dan seriously. As if I would. I bit into my pastry with a little more energy than was necessary.

"He's a good sort, our Dan," Gladys went on, as if she hadn't noticed she'd offended me. "A man like that should be married, that's what I say. T'isn't right for a good man to be alone, but there you are. Shame about his wife, though."

She paused, waiting for me to ask the obvious. I was only too happy to oblige. There'd been times when I'd wondered if he was married. Since he hadn't mentioned a wife I'd assumed he wasn't. "So what about his wife?" I asked, my mouth still full of crumbs.

"Died, didn't she. Young, she was. They'd only been married a few years. Got a blood clot in her leg and somehow it ended up in her brain. It was all over in minutes." Gladys shook her head, making her double chins wobble. "I never saw anyone so broken up as Dan was, poor bugger."

"I'm sorry," I said, my heart aching for Dan's loss.

"None of us ever thought he'd make it through that, but he did." Gladys fixed her gaze on me. "Never looked at another woman since, he hasn't. Dan's the kind of man who only ever loves like that once in his life. He'll never get over losing Ellen. He'll go to his grave still loving her, that man will."

She needn't have worried about me so much. Much as I enjoyed being with him, I knew better than to entertain those kind of thoughts. For one thing, my stay here was temporary. There could be no future in an involvement like that — even if he were interested. In a way it was a relief to know where I stood. I wasn't ready for that kind of relationship. I wasn't sure I'd ever be ready.

Though I had to admit I felt a certain sense of sadness and loss, a wistful reflection of how it must feel to be loved that much by a man like Dan Connelly.

Edward Perkins scurried out from behind his desk and held out his hand when I entered his office a while later. I returned his weak handshake and took the chair he offered.

"Well, I take it you've decided to put the cottage up for sale," he said, after exchanging the customary comments about the weather.

"Not exactly." I took a deep breath. "I've decided to rent it to the Hodges. I'd like to know what a reasonable amount would be."

He looked taken aback, but shuffled through his papers a bit before giving me a figure.

I calculated the sum back into dollars. The figure seemed high to me. I decided not to question it. "Do you have a standard contract form I can use?"

"As a matter of fact I do." He pulled a drawer open in front of him, muttering, "Somewhere . . . I think." After some scrabbling about he uttered a grunt of satisfaction. "Ah, here it is." He handed two sheets of paper over to me. "Are you quite sure you want to do this? You do realize you'll be responsible for repairs and maintenance? That might be difficult with you living so far away."

"I'm sure the Hodges and I can come to some arrangement." I folded the papers in half and tucked them into my purse.

Obviously disappointed to be deprived of his commission, he jammed his glasses higher up his nose. "Perhaps you should consult a lawyer first. Listen to your options before you make a firm decision."

No doubt he was right, but I didn't want to listen to all the reasons I shouldn't rent the cottage to Gillian and her family. This was what I wanted to do and I wasn't about to let anyone change my mind.

I needed time. Time to win Gillian over. Time to be accepted as part of the family. I wanted to be a grandmother to those adorable children, and I wanted to be a step-mother to Gillian. I wanted to be part of her life, find out what made her happy and what made her sad, listen to her dreams and her goals.

I wanted to watch Craig, Sheila and Robbie grow up into adults and forge paths in their lives. I wanted it all — more than I'd ever wanted anything in my life, and I was prepared to do anything to have it.

I left that untidy little office feeling as if I were about to dive into a swimming pool in the hopes there was water. I was giving up a substantial sum of ready cash that was supposed to finance me until I got back on my feet. I had no way of knowing if my plan would work. Gillian could hate me for the rest of her days. Or at least refuse to consider my side of the story.

Maybe I'd never have that kind of bond with any of the Hodges, but I had to try. I could not go back home without knowing I'd put everything I had into my efforts to be part of their lives. To be part of a family at last.

On my own in the traffic, I drove at a nervous crawl to the cottage. I'd called Gillian from Edward Perkins's office, and she'd agreed to see me, though I could tell she wasn't exactly brimming with enthusiasm.

As usual, her expression, when she opened the door, warned me not to expect too much from her. I followed her into the living room, praying that she'd at least accept my offer.

"I can't talk long," she said, glancing at the fireplace. "I have to be at work soon and it's a long walk."

I followed her gaze and saw a beautiful little clock with a glass dome sitting on the mantelpiece. Four golden balls spiraled inside the dome, keeping time for the decorative clock face above it. I frowned, wondering where I'd seen a clock like that before. "I can give you a lift if you like?"

"I'd rather walk, thank you." Gillian gestured at an armchair and sat down opposite me.

"It's raining," I pointed out.

"I'm used to rain."

I smiled. "So am I. It rains all winter in the Northwest."

"So when are you putting the cottage up for sale, then?" Gillian stared at her feet, which were encased in sensible brown brogues. She wore brown slacks with a floral shirt, and she'd dragged her hair back from her face with a black ribbon. With that brooding expression, she looked so much like Brandon I bit my lip to stop myself from saying so.

She looked up when I didn't answer. "I'd like to know, because I'll have to keep it tidy all the time. Ned's already looking for somewhere to rent, but I don't know how long it'll take to find somewhere we can afford."

"You could stay here," I said, trying to keep the excitement out of my voice.

Gillian shook her head. "We couldn't afford to pay rent for a house like this. We'll have to find a flat somewhere."

"What would a flat cost you to rent?"

She looked at me as if it were none of my business, but named a figure that was a little more than half the amount Perkins had suggested.

I had decided to halve Perkins's estimate anyway and gave Gillian the figure. "I'd be willing to rent the cottage to you for that sum if you want to stay."

She stared at me, her eyes widening in disbelief.

"I'm not going to sell the cottage after all," I told her. "I've decided to rent it and as tenants you have first option on it. Talk it over with your husband. You can call me at the hotel later and tell me what you've decided."

For a long moment she appeared to

struggle with indecision, then she burst out, "But nobody rents a house for that piddling amount. You'd be out of your mind. You can get a lot more for it than that."

It must have cost her to be that honest. I liked her for that. "I don't have time to wait around and interview possible tenants." I opened my purse and pulled out the rental contract. "I would rather rent it to you at a reasonable rate so that you can stay here and then the whole matter will be settled."

She seemed to be turning the offer over in her mind. "That's very generous of you, Mrs. Maitland. What do I have to do in return?"

I ignored the little stab of indignation. I really couldn't blame her for being suspicious. After all, I did have an ulterior motive, even if it was a noble one. "Well, we would have to come to some arrangements about the maintenance. Perhaps your husband would be willing to do small repairs, as long as I take care of any major ones?"

Gillian looked worried. "Well, Ned isn't good with his hands. We usually find someone on the cheap to take care of most of it. Not that much goes wrong, really."

"Good. Then it's settled?" I held out the forms to her.

She stared at them as if I were offering

her a treasure chest full of gold, then reached out and took them from me. "I'll have Ned look these over."

I got to my feet. "It's a standard contract, but if you'd rather have a lawyer look over it I'll be happy to provide one."

"I don't think we'll need that." She dropped the contract onto the table at her side and stood. "I'll see what Ned says and I'll give you a ring at the hotel."

Well satisfied, I headed for the door. If I was right about Gillian, she'd be the one making the decision. Ned would just have to go along with it.

Gillian opened the door for me, and I stepped outside. The rain had stopped, leaving a fresh smell of wet grass and salty air. "I'll wait to hear from you then," I said, as I paused to say goodbye.

She almost smiled. "I'll give you a ring this evening."

I nodded and turned away.

"Mrs. Maitland?"

I looked back at her.

"Thank you." She sounded as if she meant it.

"Please," I said, afraid to hope for too much. "Call me Marjorie."

She didn't answer, and I had to leave without knowing if I'd made a breakthrough or not. As I drove back to the hotel, I convinced myself that I'd at least taken a step forward. Heaven knows what I was going to do for money, but I intended to stay in Miles End until I'd achieved my purpose. No matter what it took.

CHAPTER 11

I put in a call to Val that afternoon. It was a little after eight in the morning in Seattle. She sounded tired when she answered the phone. "I can't sleep," she complained, when I asked her if she was okay. "This damn ankle. I miss my workouts. Men don't like flabby muscles on a woman."

I glanced over my shoulder to make sure I was alone. "I'm going to need your help," I told Val. "I need you to get some of my clothes out of storage and send them to me."

"What happened to your clothes?" Her gasp echoed down the line. "Don't tell me you were robbed?"

Good old Val. Always with the worst-case scenario. "No," I told her. "I've decided to stay here for a while longer. It's getting chilly here so I need some warmer things."

"You're staying? How long?"

"I don't know. Things are a bit complicated and —"

"Marjorie Maitland, if you don't tell me what's going on over there I'm getting the next plane."

I frowned. "Didn't you get my letter?"

"What letter?"

I realized, belatedly, that my letter couldn't possibly have reached her yet. "I wrote you a long letter explaining everything." I heard voices coming down the stairs and knew I only had a moment before someone would be able to hear me.

"Why can't you tell me now?"

"Because I'm on a public phone and I don't want to broadcast my business to everyone in the hotel."

"You don't have a phone in your room? What kind of medieval hole have you landed in? What about your cell phone?"

"I'll have to sign up for service." I flattened myself against the wall to let two women get by.

Unaware of my predicament, Val went on talking. "Why don't you get a computer so we can exchange e-mails for free? It would probably pay for itself if you're there for any length of time."

"I might just do that. Now write down this address where you can send the clothes." I paused until the women had closed the door of the dining room behind them before adding, "I'll need all my underwear, two or three sweaters, my leather jacket . . ." I went on with the list until I was sure I had everything covered.

"I'd better insure this lot," Val said when I was finished.

"I'll wire you some money." I paused. "Thanks, Val. I really appreciate this."

"Hey, what are friends for?" She paused for a moment, then added, "You are coming back here, aren't you? I mean, you're not thinking of doing something stupid like staying there permanently?"

I laughed. "Of course not. I thought I might stay until after Christmas, though. I'd like to see what the holidays are like in England."

"They don't have Thanksgiving, you know."

"Then I guess I'll have to celebrate it on my own." I ended the conversation with a promise to keep in touch with her, then decided to go back to The Tea Parlor for another Cornish pastie.

I chose to walk down. I needed the exercise. My fondness for British pastry threatened to add even more pounds to my less-than-svelte body. I couldn't face the thought of Val's lecture if I returned with all that extra weight.

There was another reason I wanted to walk, though I did my best to ignore it. Lurking in the back of my mind was the notion that there might be a chance to bump into Dan if I was on foot.

Much to my disappointment, that didn't happen, and I arrived at the tea shop out of breath and mouth watering at the prospect of my lunch.

My usual table was taken, and a young girl I didn't recognize rather sullenly showed me to a table in the dark corner by the fireplace.

At least I wasn't so much on display there, which gave me the opportunity to study the other customers as I waited for my order. My honeymoon couple were obviously enjoying lunch elsewhere, but the two women I'd noticed the day I'd had lunch with Dan sat two tables away from me, and kept glancing in my direction as they chatted back and forth.

I wondered if they were talking about me, and rejected the thought. I had to stop thinking everyone was spying on me and discussing my business behind my back.

Gladys joined me at my table just as I was about to leave. "Finally got a minute," she said, as she heaved her body onto a chair. "Been busy today, we have."

"So I noticed." I nodded at the young girl crossing the room. "You've got a new waitress?"

Gladys sighed. "Gawd knows how long she'll stay. I can't afford to pay 'em much, and they'd rather go all the way into town to work. They can earn twice as much there."

Aware that the news would reach her before the day was out, I said quietly, "I'm not going to sell the cottage after all. I've decided to rent it to Gillian."

I could see the approval in Gladys's warm gaze. "Good on you. I'm sure she was relieved."

"Yes, I think she was."

"So, does that mean you're going to leave us?"

"Well, no, actually . . . I've decided to stay around for a little while. I like being here in Miles End, it's so wonderfully peaceful."

"And you can get to know the Hodges better," Gladys said, with her usual foresight.

"Yes." I smiled at her. "You think I'm being a little too optimistic?"

"Not at all." She grinned at me, revealing her crooked yellow teeth. "I get the feeling you can do anything you set your mind on."

"I hope so. This is important to me."

I hesitated, wondering how much I should confess. "I don't have much time. The hotel isn't exactly cheap and I'll need to get back to the States and find a job pretty soon."

"Hmm." Gladys tapped her fingers on the table. "Tell you what, I've got a spare room upstairs. We'd have to share a bathroom and everything, but you're welcome to it for just a half share of the utilities if that's okay. It would help me out with the bills. I can show it to you now, if you like?"

It took me all of five seconds to consider the suggestion. "Gladys, that's wonderful." I beamed at her. "I'd love to look at it if you have time. Thank you so much."

"Come along then." She shoved down on the table and struggled to her feet. "I'll need a few days to get everything ready for you, but if you decide you want it you can move in by the end of the week. How's that?"

"That's perfect." I felt like hugging myself. The unexpected offer seemed like a sign that I was meant to stay and have the chance to work things out with Gillian. It also meant that maybe I'd be able to spend a little more time with Dan, but that was something I pushed to the back of my mind.

Right then I was too happy to know I could stay for a while longer in this lovely little village that was quickly claiming my heart.

Gladys showed me the guest room, and while it was smaller than what I was used to, it looked warm and cozy. At least the bed was wide enough to allow for my habit of sprawling in my sleep. A tall chest of drawers stood in one corner, next to a wardrobe like the one I used in the hotel. Apparently the British weren't accustomed to built-in closets.

"You've got a nice view of the village green," Gladys said, pointing at the window.

Intrigued, I went to look. I realized the room was in the back of the building and would be sheltered from the noise of local traffic. I liked that.

I peered through the lace curtains at a small, fenced-in yard below, where a line of sheets flapped in the breeze. Beyond the fence I could see the town square. A white stone monument, surrounded by hordes of chrysanthemums, stood in the middle of a large rectangle of grass. Benches were scattered about, and a beautiful gray stone church with a tall spire stood guard on one side.

A couple of women, loaded down with shopping bags, chatted to each other in front of the churchyard, while a young boy on a bike sailed past them with a little white dog yapping and chasing after him.

The whole scene seemed so tranquil, so familiar, yet so perfectly English, like a picture in a travel magazine. I smiled at the thought and turned back to Gladys. "I'll take it," I said. "If you're sure I won't get in your way."

"Not at all." Gladys's wrinkles deepened as her face glowed with pleasure. "It will be nice to have some company. Now that the winter's coming, I won't be getting too many customers. A few regulars maybe, but not enough to keep me busy all the time. Gets lonely when you've got time on your hands, don't it, dearie."

I couldn't have agreed with her more. In fact, the afternoon stretched out before me in a depressing vacuum of empty hours with nothing to do.

I arrived back at the hotel planning to call Val and tell her about the new arrangements. By the time my clothes arrived I would already have left the hotel. I needed her to send them to The Tea Parlor.

As I entered the lobby I noticed a man standing at the check-in counter. There was something familiar about the hair, the build, something . . . I just couldn't place it.

"There she is now," I heard Ernie say, and

the man spun around to face me.

Even then, I didn't remember where we'd met. I watched him walk toward me, hand outstretched, a smile warming his pleasant face.

"Marjorie! Great to see you again!"

Then I remembered. "Wes!" I shook his hand, wondering how I could have forgotten my companion on the plane in such a short time. "What are you doing here?"

"I'm on my way to a business meeting in Exeter. I had some time on my hands so I thought I'd look you up. You told me you were staying in Miles End and this is the only halfway decent hotel within miles." He took my arm and started walking me back to the door.

We were outside before I'd collected my thoughts enough to ask. "Where are we going?"

"For a drink. My car's right outside. The pub's got a comfortable little bar where we can enjoy a beer and catch up on all the news, then we can have dinner and . . ."

I was tempted. I might even have agreed if just then I hadn't seen the little red car driving past with Dan's face staring right at me. He saw me looking at him and quickly switched his focus to the road ahead.

I knew in that moment that I didn't want

to go anywhere with Wes. I pulled my arm free and said as pleasantly as I could, "I'm so sorry, Wes. I don't mean to be rude, but I have plans for this afternoon and evening."

"Oh!" He looked put out. "I thought you didn't know anybody here. That's why I came looking for you. I thought you might enjoy spending a little time with a friend."

In the first place, I wouldn't classify a few hours of conversation as a friendship. In the second place, I resented his assumption that I was so desperate for company I'd blindly follow wherever and whenever he led. That was a little too Brandon-like for me.

"Actually I've met several people since I got here," I told him. "I'm so sorry you had a wasted journey."

He made an attempt at a smile. "It's not wasted. I got to see you. How about I stop by next week on my way back —"

"I'm afraid I'll be leaving this weekend." It wasn't exactly a lie. I would be moving out of the hotel, at least.

"Oh, well, in that case . . ."

He looked thoroughly flustered now, but I couldn't feel too sorry for him. He'd taken a hell of a lot for granted. "Thank you for stopping by, and I hope your business meeting goes well." I started backing up the steps. "It was nice to see you. Goodbye,

Wes." With that I fled up the steps and back into the hotel.

Val sounded ever more grumpy when I called her a few minutes later. "I'm going crazy," she moaned. "I can't stand this sitting around. However did you stand it for all those months?"

"Not very well," I reminded her.

"Well, what's up, then? Changed your mind and you're coming home, right? I could use some help at the club now that I'm off my feet for a while."

I smiled. "Doing what? I'm not a trainer."

"No, but Angela is. She's the accountant I hired. Turns out she used to be a trainer, so she's taking over for me until I'm on my feet. So, if you're coming back and need a job . . ."

"I'm not coming back. At least, not for a while. I just have a new address where to send my clothes."

I waited through what seemed to be an unusually long pause. "What aren't you telling me?" Val demanded at last. "If I didn't know you better I'd say you've met a man and can't tear yourself away from him."

I pushed the vision of Dan out of my mind. "Ah, but you do know me better. Just have a little patience. My letter will explain everything."

"You know I don't have any patience." Her sigh trembled across six thousand miles of cable. "All right, but I'm warning you, I'll have questions."

That I didn't doubt. I hung up with her final command ringing in my ears. *Get a damn computer.*

I'd reached the steps when I heard Ernie calling out my name. I walked back to the counter, praying that Wes hadn't returned for another attempt to take me out for a drink.

"You got a message from Gillian Hodge. She wants you to give her a ring," Ernie said, his eyes brimming with curiosity.

I thanked him and scuttled away before he could ask any questions. I still had Gillian's phone number in the pocket of my slacks, which saved me going back upstairs. All that climbing up and down was taking a toll on my legs.

Gillian answered the phone on the first ring, making me suspect that she'd been waiting for my call. "We'd like to rent the house," she said, as soon as I'd greeted her. "Ned says he'll do what he can with the repairs. Like I said, he's not very good with his hands. We do know a few chaps who could help him out though."

"That sounds great." I hadn't really expected her to turn down the offer, but it was a relief to know it was settled. "I'd like to come by this evening and pick up the papers, if it's not too inconvenient?"

She hesitated just a little too long before saying, "I s'pose that'll be all right. The children go to bed about eight, if you want to wait till after that?"

"I'd really like to see them, if that's okay with you. How about seven? Will that work?"

I'd really given her no choice, but I was determined to put the second part of my plan in action as soon as possible. I wanted to win the children over, and there was no time like the present.

Gillian reluctantly agreed, and I hung up, feeling well satisfied with the way things had gone so far.

I spent the next hour or so in town doing some shopping then bought a hamburger at the fast-food restaurant before heading out for the cottage.

I arrived shortly before seven, and again Gillian opened the door promptly. This time, however, the three children stood huddled on each side of her. Ned sat in an armchair in front of the television when I walked in and barely looked up at my greeting.

Gillian offered the usual cup of tea, but I

declined. I could still feel the effects of the hamburger I'd eaten and I didn't want to add any more acid to my stomach.

"Ned, turn that telly off," Gillian ordered, as I sat down in the chair next to him.

Without a word he picked up the remote and did as she asked, then reached for the newspaper lying on the arm of his chair.

"I hope you don't mind," I said, opening the shopping bag I'd brought with me, "I picked up a couple of things for the kids."

Gillian's expression was sour, but she didn't say anything as I handed out my gifts. I'd bought a handheld electronic game for Craig, building blocks for Robbie and a small doll for Sheila.

Robbie squealed and sat down with the blocks in the middle of the room. Craig tried to look disinterested, but his eyes gleamed when he switched on the game. Sheila took the doll as if she were afraid it might break.

"What do you say?" Gillian asked sharply.

A chorus of "thank you!" answered her.

"You're welcome." I smiled at Sheila, who held the doll in one hand while she examined its clothes with the other.

"Can I have a hat for her, Mummy?" She held up the doll for her mother's inspection.

"We'll see," Gillian said, still with that disapproving look on her face.

"Mummy makes hats for dolls," Sheila explained. "She sells them at the Christmas bazaar."

"Really?" I looked up at Gillian. "What kind of hats?"

"I'll show you." Sheila darted from the room, despite a protest from her mother.

"I'd really like to see them," I said, hoping to soften that frown on Gillian's face.

"I've got the papers already signed." Gillian padded across the room on stockinged feet and picked up the papers lying on the table. "Ned and I both signed them. I hope we did it right."

I took the papers and glanced over them. They looked all right to me. I made a mental note to show them to James when I got back home, just in case there was something that needed to be changed. "This is fine," I said. "I'm glad we could come to an agreement."

"When do we pay the first month's rent?" Gillian asked. "You didn't have anything written down on that."

Realizing October was just days away, I decided to give her time to save the money. "How about the first of November? Will that work for you?"

She nodded, her expression softening just a bit. "Thank you."

She looked as if she wanted to say something else, but just then Sheila burst back into the room holding a large square box in her hands.

"Here they are!" She turned the box upside down and dumped a pile of fabric objects into my lap.

Gillian protested again, but I paid no attention to her. I picked up one of the hats and turned it around in my fingers. It was an old-fashioned hat, the kind women wore at the turn of the twentieth century. The wide velvet brim was covered with delicate little pink roses, tiny lavender ribbon bows and swathes of pink chiffon.

"This is exquisite," I exclaimed, as I held the beautiful piece of work up to the light.

"Can I have one for my dolly?" Sheila asked, tugging at her mother's sweater.

"All right. Pick one out then put the rest back," Gillian told her.

Sheila came and stood at my knee. "Which one shall I have?"

Thoroughly charmed that she'd asked my advice, I held up another gorgeous hat decorated with miniature butterflies and yellow ribbons. "This one is lovely." I reached for yet another treasure. "Or this one."

In the end we examined every hat in my lap before settling on the one with the butterflies, which happily fit the doll I'd brought her.

All the time Gillian pretended to be absorbed in helping Robbie fit his blocks together, though I knew she watched us out of the corner of her eye.

Once we had the hat settled firmly on the doll's blond curls, Gillian announced it was time to get ready for bed. The children's protests were ignored, and after some prodding, Robbie piled all his blocks back into the box.

Sheila thanked me again for her doll. "I'm going to call her Patsy," she told me, and I agreed that was a very good name for a doll.

Even Craig gruffly thanked me before saying good-night, and Robbie completely stole my heart when he threw his chubby arms around my neck and hugged me.

I could have held his sturdy little body forever, but with regret I let him go, with a promise I'd come back soon to see him.

Throughout all this Ned hadn't said a word to me, but had remained buried behind his newspaper.

As Gillian disappeared upstairs with the children, I said awkwardly, "Thank you for agreeing to help with the repairs and maintenance."

He lowered the paper and peered at me over the top of it. "Can't promise much. I'm not much good at mending things."

"That's all right." I smiled at him. "I'm sure we'll muddle through between us."

He nodded. "The missus usually takes care of all that."

I could see what Gladys meant about Gillian doing everything. I was still trying to think of something else to say to him when Gillian came back into the room.

"Well, I'd better be going." I got to my feet. "I've enjoyed my visit. I hope you'll allow me to come back and see the children again sometime? I really loved visiting with them."

Without answering me, Gillian walked to the front door and opened it.

I had a nasty feeling in my stomach that had nothing to do with the hamburger.

As I reached her, she said quietly, "Thank you for the toys, Mrs. Maitland, but I really think it would be better if you didn't see the children. I don't want them getting attached to you. You'll be going back to America soon and they've already lost a grandmother. It would be too hard on them if they got to like you and then had to lose you again."

I couldn't believe she meant it. I stared at her, silently begging her to take back the words, even though I knew that whatever I said, nothing would change her mind. It wasn't so much what was in her eyes, as what was missing. No compassion, no apology, only a blank stare.

I felt as if she'd offered me a glimpse of something warm and precious, only to snatch it away again. My hands were cold, and my entire body ached with an odd feeling of emptiness that surpassed anything I'd felt over losing Brandon.

Searching for words that might heal the void, all I could manage was a husky goodnight. Then I left, with the bitter taste of defeat in my mouth.

CHAPTER 12

I drove back to the hotel in a haze of misery. To be struck down on my first attempt was a bitter blow. I should have known it wasn't going to be that easy.

The problem was, I could see Gillian's point. She didn't want the children to go through another loss of a grandparent, even if I was a surrogate. To the children it would make no difference.

Thinking about it, however, it occurred to me that Robbie, at least, had to be too young to remember Eileen.

I frowned. Was Gillian making that an excuse for not having to see me again? If so, I wasn't about to give up that easily. I'd just have to find another way to break through that wall of hostility. Though right then I couldn't imagine how I was going to go about it.

I still hadn't come up with a solution when I moved into my little room over the tea shop that weekend. I'd had to park my car in a garage down the high street, since parking outside was only temporary. I'd arranged for cell-phone service, which delighted Val when I called to tell her.

She'd received my letter and spent ten precious minutes asking endless questions, to which I had no answers.

"So tell me about this guy, Dan," she said, when I told her all I could about Gillian and her family. "I just know there's more to it than what you said in your letter. Is he a young guy? What's he like? Has he got money?"

I sighed. "Dan's just a casual acquaintance who gave me a ride a couple of times, that's all. I've rented a car now so I probably won't see him again."

"Uh-huh," Val said, in obvious disbelief. "Tell that to the marines."

I deliberately changed the subject and asked about the club, ending the conversation with a promise to call back soon. I didn't want to talk about Dan. I'd postponed our date to visit the castle. I wasn't exactly sure why, but I felt I needed time to get myself settled again before I could relax and enjoy the encounter with him.

Maybe I felt a little wary about him seeing me with Wes, though there was absolutely no reason why I should. Or maybe, after learning about Dan's devotion to his late wife, I was concerned I might enjoy his company just a little too much.

In any case, when I'd called to ask for a rain check, he'd sounded a little abrupt. He'd seemed surprised when I told him I was moving into the tea shop. I couldn't tell if he was happy about it or not. That left a bad feeling under my ribs for a couple of days before I convinced myself I was being way too immature.

I spent the weekend rearranging the room and exploring the rest of the village. A cold October wind pummeled my cheeks as I sat on a bench on the village green. A few yards away a small boy struggled with a kite, getting entangled in the string in the process.

It reminded me of Seattle and my day in the park, when I watched children play and wondered if I'd ever laugh again. So much had happened since that day. So much had changed.

If only I could work things out with Gillian.

I sat for a long time thinking about how I could reach my stepdaughter, while the leaves swirled around me and the shouts of children echoed over the damp grass.

Across the green an impatient mother hauled her small daughter along by her hand. A doll dangled in the child's other hand, its feet almost scraping the ground.

I watched them hurry away, and as the first cold drops of rain stung my face, the idea came to me. It would be a long shot, but certainly worth a try.

I couldn't wait to get back to the tea shop, and a few minutes later I arrived there breathless, with my hair whipping across my eyes. The door opened just as I reached for it, and I had to drag the hair out of my face to see.

Dan stared right back at me, his expression hard to read. "Missed me again," he said, and although he sounded cheerful enough, there was an odd look in his eyes that unsettled me.

"Practice makes perfect," I sang out, trying to disguise the sudden tightening in my throat.

I expected another teasing comment from him, but instead, he gave me a mock salute and took off down the street. My good humor vanished. I stepped inside the tearoom feeling as if I'd just lost something important.

It was late afternoon, and the tearoom was empty of customers. As I crossed to the stairs that would take me to my room Gladys called out to me from the kitchen.

"I've just made a pot of tea, dearie, if you want one?"

"No thanks. I'm going down to get my car in a few minutes." I started up the stairs. "I'm going to see Gillian."

Gladys came out into the hallway and stood at the foot of the stairs. "Did you say something to upset Dan?"

I paused, though I didn't turn around to look at her. "Not as far as I know. Why?"

"I dunno. He just seemed a bit off, that's all."

"Perhaps he's not feeling well." I took another step up.

"You're not giving him the cold shoulder because of what I said about his wife, are you?"

This time I did turn around. "Of course not. I like Dan. I feel bad that he lost his wife, but that has nothing to do with me, or my friendship with him."

Gladys gave me one of her shrewd looks. "Okay. I was just wondering, that's all."

She started back to the kitchen, but I couldn't let it go at that. I called out to her. "Why, what did he say?"

"Oh, nothing much. I asked him how he enjoyed your visit to the castle and he said he thought you'd found someone else to show you around."

She disappeared through the door and I stared after her, my pulse quickening. That sounded a lot like jealousy. No, that was ridiculous. Hadn't Gladys just told me he was still in love with his wife? I shook my head and went back up the stairs. Wishful thinking, that's all it was.

I pulled off my sweater and changed it for a shirt and a jacket, then ran back down the stairs, my good humor restored. Dan obviously wanted to take me to the castle, and I was more than ready to oblige. I promised myself I'd call him as soon as I'd talked to Gillian.

I'd decided not to call her first, half-afraid she'd refuse to see me. I expected her to be annoyed with me for turning up on her doorstep without notice, but she was her usual stoic self when she invited me in.

I turned down her offer of tea, and launched into my speech. "I've been thinking about those beautiful dolls' hats you make. I know you sell them at a Christmas bazaar, but have you thought about selling them commercially? In a shop, I mean. There are quite a few gift shops in Stattenham that I'm sure would love to have them, and you could deliver them say . . . once a month, and I'm pretty sure you'd make enough money on them to help pay your rent."

I paused for breath, my heart sinking when I saw Gillian shake her head.

"I don't think so." She shifted her attention to the living-room window. "I don't drive, you see. I couldn't deliver them."

"Oh."

It had never occurred to me that a woman her age wouldn't be able to drive. I was about to offer to deliver the hats myself when she added, "Even if I could, I haven't got a car, and even if I did, I couldn't make enough of the hats to sell in the shops."

"You have quite a lot already," I pointed out.

"They're for the bazaar." She hesitated, then flicked a glance at me. "Thank you for thinking of it, though."

"Perhaps you have some friends who could help you make them," I suggested, reluctant to give up what I thought was a brilliant idea.

"All the women I know are busy with their own stuff."

Something about the way the words came out made me think she didn't have too many friends. Which made me all the more determined to become one. "Well, I'm no good at sewing," I said, "but I'd be more

206

than willing to deliver the hats for you, if you'd like."

She lifted her chin and gave me the first direct stare since I'd arrived. "Why?"

Taken by surprise, I stumbled over my answer. "Well . . . ah . . . I just think the hats are so beautiful, and they'd make wonderful souvenirs and gifts, and I thought it would give you extra cash —"

"I don't need extra cash." Now she looked defiant. "We do all right, Ned and me. We don't need much. Ned's happy as long as he has his beer and telly, and the children have good food and clothes. That's all we need."

I didn't want to say so, but looking around that living room, I thought there were quite a few things they needed. The furniture was obviously old and quite worn, not to mention the threadbare curtains at the window. Judging from the children's excitement when I gave them their gifts, I figured they didn't have a lot of toys to play with.

As if reading my mind, Gillian said abruptly, "You've been generous enough, Mrs. Maitland, giving us a decent rent. I couldn't accept anything else from you."

Maybe not, but the kids would. The thought gave me the courage to say, "About the children. I'd really like to see more of them while I'm here. If I promise to keep in touch with them when I go back — you know, send them a gift for birthdays and Christmas, write letters to them — would you mind if I came by now and then?" I gave her my warmest smile. "Maybe one day, when they're a little older, you could all visit me in the States. I'm sure they'd enjoy that."

I could see she was torn. Not for herself. She'd made that plain enough. But I could tell the possible benefits to her children in having a benevolent surrogate grandparent in the U.S. obviously appealed to her.

After what seemed a painfully long pause, she said grudgingly, "Well, I s'pose it wouldn't hurt. Just as long as it's at the weekends. I don't want their schooldays interrupted. They have homework to do and then they go to bed early. Children that age need their sleep."

"I couldn't agree more." I got to my feet, satisfied that I'd taken a giant leap forward. "Thank you, Gillian. I'll stop by on Saturday?"

She nodded, and showed me to the door.

"By the way," I said, determined to press my advantage. "Mrs. Maitland is such a mouthful for the little ones. Do you think they could call me Marjorie?"

I didn't have the nerve to ask that they call me Grandma, so I was totally floored when Gillian said, "How about Nana? Would that be all right?"

I had to clear my throat before I could answer her. "I'd like that very much," I said quietly.

"All right, then." She opened the door, and I sailed out of there feeling as if I'd just conquered the world.

I called Dan as soon as I got back to my room. My disappointment when he didn't answer was way out of proportion, and I had to remind myself again not to let my emotions rule my common sense. I left a message and gave him my cell-phone number. Now it was up to him if he still wanted to go to the castle.

Gladys had closed the tea shop and I could hear the TV blaring out in the living room. I wasn't in the mood for whatever game show she was watching, so I walked down to the garage to get my car.

I thought I might drive along the coast a little ways and take a look at the lighthouse. Gladys had told me it was supposed to be haunted, and I was intrigued enough to want to explore.

I had just pulled out into the high street when my cell phone played its bouncy little tune. *Val,* I thought, and reluctantly flipped it open. Dan's voice answered me, almost sending me into the sidewalk. I pulled over and set the brake.

"Sorry I missed your call," Dan said, while I sat there with the phone jammed against my ear in fear I'd miss something important. "I was out on a job."

"I just thought I'd reschedule our trip to the castle." I hesitated, then said in a rush, "That's if you still want to go."

"Of course I still want to go." His voice sounded odd, more restrained somehow.

I gripped the phone harder. "Okay, so when's a good time?"

"How about now?"

I looked at my watch. "Aren't they closed?"

He laughed, relaxing my tense nerves. "It's open all the time. There's nothing in there to steal. Just broken-down walls and steps. You were probably expecting suits of armor, massive portraits and velvet curtains, right?"

"Something like that," I admitted.

"Sorry to disappoint you."

The thought flashed through my mind that nothing could disappoint me when I was with him, but I clamped down on that. "No, really, I'd still like to see it. It is old, isn't it?"

"Dates back to somewhere around the seventh century."

The thought of anything lasting that long astounded me. "Then I'd definitely like to see it."

"We'll have to leave now before it gets too dark. I'll pick you up in five minutes."

I sounded a little breathless when I answered him. "I'm in my car. Why don't I come and get you?"

He barely hesitated before answering. "I'm down by the harbor. Just past the warehouses. You can't miss it. Shabby blue building. Has my name over the door."

"I'll find it." I closed the phone and pulled out into the street. Five minutes later I coasted along in front of the warehouses. The blue building Dan had described sat at the very end of them, with just enough parking in front for two cars. I pulled up, trying to decide if I should wait in the car or go ring the doorbell.

The decision was made for me when the door to the building opened and Dan stepped out, turning to lock the door before sauntering over to me.

I was prepared to slide over and let him take the wheel, but he came around to the passenger side and climbed into the seat next to me. Brandon had never trusted me to drive. The fact that Dan took it for granted made me like him all the more.

I headed out the coast road toward the castle, more excited about being with Dan than exploring an ancient relic, despite my best efforts to control my wayward emotions.

"I thought you might have seen it already," Dan said, as we sped along the shoreline.

I sent him a quick glance, but his expression told me nothing about what he was thinking. I tried to sound innocent. "Oh? What made you think that?"

"The chap I saw you with the other day. American, wasn't he?"

Gleefully I realized he was probing for information. "How did you know?"

"The crew cut gave him away. And the suit. American businessman, I'd say."

"Very clever." I waited just long enough to sound casual when I added, "I met him on the plane coming over here. He was going into Exeter for a business meeting and looked me up."

Dan took his time answering, too. "Oh. I thought you might be old friends or something."

"Just casual acquaintances, that's all." It was on the tip of my tongue to tell him I'd refused Wes's offer to take me to dinner, but thought better of it. I didn't want to attach too much importance to the fact that Dan had apparently given some thought to my relationship with another man.

Nevertheless, if I could have taken my hands off the wheel just then I would have hugged myself.

Dan was right, the castle was a bit of a letdown. I don't know what I'd expected, but I found the cold stone walls and empty rooms with their slim windows depressing.

Once more I tried to imagine it as it must have looked centuries ago, but it was hard to put my knights in armor and ladies in silk gowns into the chilling, creepy remains of what once had been a mighty fortress.

Even so, I was intrigued by the deep curves carved into the stone steps by thousands of feet traipsing up and down. How I would have loved to meet some of the people who, centuries ago, must have climbed these very stairs.

Dan took me down to the dungeons, and we stood in the dark, looking up at the tiny slit of daylight yards above our head. His voice echoed around the dismal chamber when he spoke. "Can you imagine being shut up in this miserable hole for years on end? It could drive you mad."

I shivered. "I don't even want to think

about it. It's enough to give me nightmares."

"Sorry. I should have warned you."

I could see nothing when I looked in the direction of his voice. After staring at that crack of light, the contrast made the darkness all the more dense.

He spoke again, making me jump. "Let's get out of here. I'm getting hungry."

I heard him moving away and for a terrifying second I envisioned being left behind in that awful place. I leaped forward in the direction of his voice. Unfortunately, he hadn't moved as far as I'd thought. I crashed right into him.

I heard his muffled grunt, and then I stumbled. He steadied me by grabbing hold of my arms.

"Oh, great," I mumbled, as my cheeks heated up. "I'm sorry. I thought you were across the room and I was scared of being left alone. . . ." My voice trailed off. I became acutely conscious of his hands warm on my arms.

He sounded strange, too, when he answered. "I'd never do that to you. I'd never leave you alone."

All at once I couldn't breathe. Panic attack, I told myself. The bleak depths of the dungeons were getting to me. I pulled back and Dan let me go. Then he unsettled me all over again when he found my hand and led me from that desolate room that had suddenly become such a very special place.

CHAPTER 13

Minutes later we emerged into the dwindling daylight and Dan let go of my hand. He was quiet as I drove back toward the village. I longed to know what was going on in his mind.

A light mist hung over the coastline, and the sky had turned red above the hills as we reached the harbor. I pulled up outside Dan's building, sad that the jaunt was over so soon.

"I was thinking of going up to the Unicorn for a bite to eat," he said, when I cut the engine. "How about it?"

It took me a moment to realize he meant the pub on the hill, and that he was inviting me along. Flustered, I tried to sound cool and collected. "Oh, well, I hadn't really made any plans for dinner. . . ."

"Good. Then let's go. That's if you don't mind driving?"

I smiled. "Of course not. I can use the

practice. I'm still having trouble staying on the left side of the road."

"Which is the right side, of course." He smiled back, and for a long moment we just sat there, smiling at each other, with our little world inside the car turning cozy and warm.

I drove up to the pub in a haze of mixed emotions. There was no doubt in my mind that Dan and I had stepped across some kind of line, but what it meant I was too afraid to question. I kept warning myself over and over that I was becoming too attached to this man, and that it could only end in more heartbreak for me.

No matter how hard I tried, I couldn't rid myself of the excitement that kept my pulse racing as I sat opposite him in a quiet corner of the pub.

I'd always imagined British pubs to be smoky places with loud music and noisy people cheering around a dartboard. The Merry Unicorn, to give it its full name, couldn't have been more different from my vision. In fact, it would have seemed quite at home on a busy downtown Seattle street.

I could hear music, but it was the soft, nightclub kind. While the pub was obviously old, it had been renovated inside to the most modern standards.

The oak paneling, the white, lace-trimmed tablecloths and the miniature oil lamps made the room feel so cozy. While we waited for the beef Wellington Dan had ordered I noticed rows of round brass ornaments hanging on the wall. "What are those things?" I asked Dan. "I've seen them in a lot of the shops. They seem to be very popular."

Dan followed my gaze. "Horse brasses. The gypsies used to attach them to the horse's harness to keep the evil spirits away. If you look at them you'll see they're all different. Those cutout patterns can be anything from coats of arms or famous people to historic places and all kinds of animals. People collect them and hang them up over the fireplace. Some people think they bring them luck."

"Fascinating." I stared harder at them. "They look old."

"They probably are. Horse brasses have been around since the eighteenth century, and you're probably looking at genuine ones."

"They're not all genuine?"

He shook his head. "They turn them out in factories now for souvenirs. Most of them never come close to being on a horse."

The waiter, resplendent in a red shirt and

black vest, brought our order just then and I turned my attention to the delicious-looking meal in front of me.

It wasn't until we were enjoying the extra-strong coffee the British seemed to love that I brought up the subject of Dan's wife.

"Gladys told me you lost your wife soon after you were married. I'm sorry. That must have been hard." I sat stirring my coffee and didn't look up straight away.

His long silence touched a nerve, however. When I did finally look at him, the anguish in his eyes shocked me. I hunted about in my mind for another subject, frightened by the ghosts I'd conjured up for him.

Before I could say anything else, he said quietly, "It was very hard. The hardest part of it was that I didn't have time to say good-bye. She was dead by the time I got to the hospital."

A pang of remorse kept me speechless for a moment. I should never have mentioned it, I thought frantically. I'd brought up what was obviously still a very painful subject.

His sigh seemed to tremble in the air, and my heart ached for him. "Ellen was quite a woman. I wonder why it is the best ones have to die so soon."

Again I was at a loss for words. Anything that came to mind would only sound trite.

"She knew how to love," Dan went on, "with all her heart, body and soul. Not many women can do that."

I understood then. Gladys was right. Ellen was Dan's one and only, and any other woman would be second best. I felt desperately sad — for both of us.

Much to my dismay the mood was broken, and although Dan tried, I could tell his attempts at humor were forced. The night had turned cold when we stepped out into the parking lot, and I shivered.

"I hope you brought a coat with you," Dan said, as we walked toward the car. "Devon's winter is milder than the rest of the country but it can still get cold at night."

"I'm having one sent over." I dug into my purse for my keys.

"You must be planning on staying a while." He opened the door for me and held it while I climbed in behind the wheel.

"For a while, yes." I figured he already knew my plans if he'd talked to Gladys, but decided to tell him anyway. I waited until he'd fastened his seat belt, then I switched on the engine.

"I'm renting the cottage to Gillian," I said, as the motor settled to a quiet hum. "I won't be selling it after all."

As I expected, he nodded. "So Gladys told

me. I bet Gillian was relieved."

"She seemed to be." I put the gear in reverse and backed the car out. "I decided to hang around for a while just to see how things go."

"Gillian's a hard nut to crack, but if anyone can get through that hard shell, I bet you can."

"Well, thank you. I'll take that as a compliment."

"It was meant as one."

Warmed by his words, I relaxed my hands on the wheel. "I'm hoping to stay until at least after Christmas. I'd love to spend the holidays in the English countryside."

"I hope you won't be disappointed. It'll probably be dull compared to Christmas in your city."

I laughed. "Somehow I don't think I'll miss all those Santas ringing bells in my face on every corner, or the endless ads blaring on TV. It's no wonder so many of us go into debt over the holidays. It's hard to resist all the stuff they throw at you."

"Commercialized, huh?"

"Very."

"Well, there's a certain amount of that here, but on a very small scale. Christmas in Miles End is more focused on singing carols in church, getting together with the family to exchange presents and eating too much. The pubs do a roaring trade, of course."

"It sounds wonderful." I let out a sigh. "Christmas should be for families."

"If you've got one."

"You don't have any family?"

"I do, but my parents and two sisters are all in Australia. Emigrated there about ten years ago. I was building up the business and decided not to go. I have a couple of aunts, but one lives in Scotland and the other in London."

"I'm sorry. You must miss them. Your parents and sisters, I mean."

"I'm used to being on my own. What about you? You must have family in America."

"Nope. My father died when I was small, and my mother a few years later. No brothers or sisters, I'm afraid."

"Your husband's family?"

I shook my head. "All gone."

He was silent for a moment, then murmured, "Things must seem very different here than what you're used to."

"No comparison. Everything is smaller here. The narrow streets, the tiny houses . . . sometimes I feel as if I'm walking around a model village."

"I can see why that would bother you."

"Oh, no, I love it. It's so quiet and peaceful. I love waking up to hear birds singing instead of traffic roaring past my window. I haven't heard a police siren since I arrived. Though I have to admit, it's a bit unsettling to see the sun rise out of the ocean instead of setting in it."

"Ah, well, if that's all, I can take you into Cornwall and you can watch the sun set in the sea."

I was sure he was just making conversation, but even so, I couldn't quite steady my pulse. "Is it far?"

"A couple of hours by car."

A moment later I pulled up in front of his building, surprised at how fast we'd arrived. "Thank you for dinner. I enjoyed it very much."

"So did I."

I wanted to say something about paying the next time, but I was afraid to take anything for granted. Besides, he'd mentioned cooking dinner for him as a payback, and I wasn't ready to be alone in his home with him. I had feelings I needed to get sorted out first.

I was relieved and sad at the same time when he said a little awkwardly, "I'd better get along and let you get home. Thanks for the lift."

"It was the least I could do."

He opened the car door and climbed out, then poked his head in to say good-night. "I'll probably see you in the tea shop."

He was gone before I could think of a way to answer him.

I drove back up the hill, passing the Unicorn once more. Light pooled from the windows and the huge lanterns in front of the door. It looked warm and cozy, and the strange ache I felt under my ribs as I left it behind made no sense at all.

Gladys had apparently gone to bed when I got back to the tea shop. The living room was silent and dark. I crept up the stairs, wincing at every creak and groan.

My room felt cold, and I thought about taking a hot bath. Like the hotel, Gladys had no shower facilities, but after all this time without one I was getting used to soaking in a tub.

Unfortunately, the pipes were old, and every time hot water ran through them it sounded like a kid learning to play drums. Bathing would have to wait until the morning.

I slid into bed, shivering as my feet contacted the icy sheets. I'd have to wear socks to bed if it got any colder. The building was heated by radiators, and Gladys turned them off at night. She'd told me she warmed her sheets with a hot-water bottle. Right then it sounded like a good idea.

I took a long time to go to sleep that night. Memories of the evening kept replaying in my mind. I couldn't forget the look in Dan's eyes when I'd mentioned Ellen.

I wished I could see a picture of her, then was glad I couldn't. I was angry for caring, then convinced myself that I would have felt as badly for anyone who'd lost the love of his life.

I lay in the dark for a long time, not sure if it was the cold that kept me awake, or the memory of Dan's hands warm on my arms.

My clothes arrived the next week, and just in time. The weather turned cold and damp, and without the central heating I was used to, I had trouble falling asleep at night.

Gladys introduced me to the hot-water bottle, which made the chilly depths of my bed bearable, until the middle of the night when I'd wake up with a bag of freezing water tucked under my knees.

Desperate for news of my hometown, I bought a used computer that I saw advertised in the local paper. It meant driving to Stattenham to pick it up, but the joy of connecting once more to the U.S. made it well worthwhile.

Val was ecstatic, of course, and for the first few days sent lengthy e-mails rambling on about her latest conquests. Since some of them were X-rated, I deleted them as soon I read them, though I was sure Gladys couldn't turn the machine on, much less access my e-mails.

She was, however, immensely interested in how much news could be exchanged with a large group of people at one time, and I had to promise I'd show her how everything worked. Since business had dropped off considerably, we had plenty of time to play.

"How did you learn all this?" Gladys asked, when I flipped through the basic functions of the computer.

"Mostly by experimenting," I admitted. I showed her how to read the local news, and lost her for five minutes while she avidly consumed every story.

"I could spend all day on this," she declared, after we'd played a couple of hands of solitaire. "It's bloody marvelous."

It was hard for me to understand how anyone ran a business without a computer, but then everyone in Miles End seemed to be years behind the times. I wondered if Dan owned one, and was tempted to do an internet search for him, but decided that had better wait until I was alone again.

I hadn't seen him in almost a week, and I missed him. Gladys mentioned that he'd been in the shop. I wondered if he was trying to avoid me, then realized I'd spent a good deal of time in my room since I'd bought the computer. Maybe he thought I was trying to avoid him.

There was one way to find out, and it was something I'd thought about ever since I'd brought the computer home. I waited until I could drag Gladys's attention away from the solitaire game.

"I've been thinking," I said, "that we could put all your bookkeeping on the computer. I know you spend about an hour or so every day working on the books. It would be much faster on this, and I'd be happy to set it up for you. I'll even keep the accounts up-to-date if you like. Then I won't feel so guilty about the low rent for my room."

Gladys's eyes widened. "You'd do that for me?"

"Of course! I'd enjoy it. It will give me something to do." After all, I had all week, since Gillian insisted I limit my visits to the weekends. I intended to extend that limit, but I was treading slowly, wary of upsetting the delicate connection between us.

So far I'd enjoyed two weekend visits with the kids. The last one had been rewarding in that I'd gotten Craig interested in my ghost stories stolen from a TV series I used to watch in the States.

Halloween was just a few days away, and I'd gotten Gillian's approval to take the children trick-or-treating. I was fascinated to learn that only in the past ten years had the South of England reinstated this ritual, having abandoned it for more than a century in favor of Guy Fawkes celebration. Effigies of the famous ancient terrorist, who was captured in the act of attempting to blow up the Houses of Parliament, were burned on huge fires, and fireworks were set off all across the countryside.

I had yet to experience this British custom and looked forward to sharing my first "Bonfire night" with the grandkids.

Gladys accepted my offer to take charge of her accounts, and I was horrified to find out how close to the edge she lived during the off-season. I tackled her about it as we sat enjoying a pot of tea one afternoon in her tiny living room.

"You don't get many customers in the winter months," I said, warming my hands on the steaming cup of tea.

"Off-season's always bad." She curled her

finger though the handle of her cup. "I'm usually holding my breath waiting for the spring when the visitors come back."

"Have you ever thought of providing dinner? There aren't many places to eat around here. Except for the hotel dining room, which is always filled, and the Unicorn, which is expensive. I'd think there'd be plenty of people looking for somewhere different to eat out."

"They're not much for eating out around here." Gladys sipped her tea and put the cup back in the saucer. "They've got Wimpy's down the road, and the fish-and-chip shop if they fancy something different."

"But that's fast food." I leaned forward, caught up in my own excitement. "You could provide something in between. Maybe just on a Friday or Saturday night to begin with. Get in a few bottles of wine. You'd make a lot of money on that alone."

Lines creased her forehead as she squinted at me. "I'm not much of a dinner cook."

"Of course you are. Anyone who can make those delicious pasties can cook a dinner. It doesn't have to be a gourmet meal." I caught my breath as an idea occurred to me. "Why don't we have a Thanksgiving dinner! I can tell you what to cook, and we'll advertise it as an American night out. We wouldn't have to charge that much and we'd still make a profit."

Gladys stared at me as if I'd suggested we climb Mount Everest. "We don't have Thanksgiving. It's an American thing."

"I know, but wouldn't it be fun? Just to see how it goes?" I waved a hand in the direction of the dining room. "Isn't it better than letting that sit empty all winter?" I took a deep breath. "I'll supervise if you like. I've cooked enough Thanksgiving dinners. We'll need the girls of course, but we could pay them a little extra. You know there is a connection, since the Pilgrims left England for America."

"I'm not sure that's a reason for celebrating."

"Maybe not. But it's a good reason to eat a fantastic dinner."

"I suppose it couldn't hurt." She frowned. "I just hope we don't get all that food in and nobody comes. That would be a terrible waste."

"That's why we'll take reservations." I felt like jumping up and down on my chair. "I'll make flyers and we'll give them out to everyone. This will be great. You'll see."

There were many times in the following month when I wondered if I'd been in my right mind when I suggested an American Thanksgiving dinner. The flyers turned out reasonably well, but some of the comments I got when I handed them out seriously undermined my confidence.

"We don't celebrate Thanksgiving in November," one crusty old gentleman informed me. "We celebrate it on September sixth.

Surprised, I asked innocently, "Really? Why then?"

"Because that's when they left." He grunted and stomped off, leaving me staring after him.

All this activity kept me in the tearoom most of the day. Since Dan came in almost every morning for tea and Danish, I got to spend a lot more time with him. We exchanged jokes, commented on the weather and passed on harmless gossip about the residents of Miles End.

I found out he was two years younger than me and I told him about my job at the health club. That was the extent of our personal conversation, and I wasn't sure if I was relieved or disappointed. It made things more simple, I guess, and that was the most I could expect. I told myself that the sooner I accepted that, the happier I'd be.

CHAPTER 14

Much to my delight and Gladys's utter astonishment, we sold out reservations for two sittings of Thanksgiving dinner. The cramped space in Gladys's kitchen limited us, and we decided that a set meal at a specific time would be easier to control. Two sittings were the best we could manage, since Gladys's fridge was too small to accommodate much. We would have to pick up most of the food that morning and store it in the pantry, which thanks to the lack of central heating was almost as cold as the fridge.

Dan offered his help in decorating the dining room, and Gillian came through with bright orange-and-green paper chains that made the whole place look festive. Even the grandchildren got into the act, copying my unprofessional drawings of pumpkins and Pilgrim hats and cutting them out to hang in the windows.

Gillian had told me they couldn't afford to come to the dinner, but after I talked to Gladys we agreed they should come as our guests. When I told Gillian about our offer I thought at first she was going to turn it down.

It was a Saturday evening, and I was on the floor playing Snakes and Ladders with the kids. Gillian sat on one armchair, working on her dolls' hats, and Ned sat on the other, lost in the TV as usual.

In all the times I'd visited them, Ned had spoken to me only twice. I never saw him speak to the kids at all, except to say goodnight when they went to bed. Gillian seemed to ignore him altogether, and acted as if he weren't there.

It irritated me that Ned neglected them that way. I thought how lucky he was to have such a wonderful family, and that he was abusing that privilege. They deserved better. The kids needed a father, just as Gillian deserved a husband.

True, she ruled the household, but what else could she do? Someone had to pick up the slack. Marriage should be a partnership, I thought. Working together, not against each other. Nobody knew better than I how utterly miserable that could be.

Intent on giving Gillian at least something

to look forward to, I told her what Gladys and I had decided. "We very much want all of you to be there," I told her. "You are family, after all. That's what Thanksgiving is all about. We had some spots left over, and they'll only go to waste if you don't fill them."

I didn't really expect her to believe that, but I thought it might make her feel less of a charity case.

She didn't answer me right away, but kept jabbing her needle in and out of the mound of velvet that would soon be transformed into a flawless work of art.

"I think the children would enjoy it," I ventured.

"I wanna go!" Robbie whined, and Sheila joined in.

"Yeah, I wanna go, too!"

Craig looked at me out of the corner of his eye.

"Wouldn't it be fun to eat turkey and stuffing and pumpkin pie?" I smiled at him. "There'll even be a small gift for all the children." I was shamelessly bribing him, of course, and since I'd just then thought of the gift idea my bank account was about to take a nosedive. There were eighteen children booked for dinner.

"I don't like turkey," Craig muttered, and

picked up the dice cup.

"We'll have ham, too. You like ham?"

Craig rattled the dice and threw it on the board. "Yeah, I s'pose so."

I tried again. "What about cherry pie?"

Both Sheila and Robbie drowned out Craig's answer with an enthusiastic "Yeah!"

I glanced at Gillian, and she had the resigned look on her face that meant she was about to cave in. Ned was still fixed on the television, and seemed oblivious of the conversation going on around him.

I figured it was time to get him involved. I raised my voice to be heard above the background music. "What do you think, Ned?"

All three kids turned their heads to look at him. Gillian's needle still stabbed in and out, but I could tell by her expression she was tensed for his reply.

"I don't care," he said, without bothering to tear his eyes away from the flickering screen in front of him.

I was just in time to catch the wry twist of Gillian's mouth. I knew what it meant. It was just what she'd expected from him.

All at once I was angry. Didn't the man know what he was doing? How dare he treat his family like invisible servants, there only for his needs and nothing else. I wanted to say something, but I couldn't bear to take away the excitement in the faces of those children. So I kept quiet. But I made up my mind that the first opportunity I got, I was going to have a little chat with Gillian.

The day before the Thanksgiving dinner, Gladys and I were going over the menu one last time when Dan arrived for his morning snack.

"Wow, this looks brilliant," he said, when he read the list. "I'm going to starve myself today so I'll have room for all this."

I laughed. "We Americans do know how to eat. I'll miss the cranberry sauce and sweet potatoes, though. I asked in the grocery store and they sent me to the produce store, but they didn't have them, either."

"She means the greengrocers," Gladys said.

"Ah, more of that splintered English you Yanks speak." Dan shook his head. "And here I was under the impression we spoke the same language."

"We do. Only our version is less complicated. Our grocers aren't green, and we don't have fishmongers or ironmongers, and we don't buy yarn in a wool shop."

"Look what you're missing."

I grinned. "You're right. Shopping in

Miles End is an adventure."

Later that afternoon, just as Gladys was taking the last pies out of the oven, Dan poked his head around the kitchen door. "Whatever that is that smells so good," he said, sniffing the air, "I want a piece of it."

"Then you'll have to wait until tomorrow." Gladys handed me the hot cherry pie and bent over to reach for another one.

Dan sidled in, hiding something behind his back. "What will it take to pinch a piece of that pie?"

"More than anything you've got," I told him.

"Yeah? Well, how about this then?" He swung a plastic bag at me.

Puzzled, I looked inside and saw fresh cranberries and sweet potatoes. I let out a whoop of delight. "Dan! This is great! Where did you get them?"

"I ran over to Stattenham. They have a big supermarket there, and I found them in there."

Touched that he'd gone to all that trouble, I did something I would never have done six months earlier. I leaned over and planted a kiss on his cheek. "Thank you," I said, giving him a smile. "That was very sweet of you."

He looked startled for a moment, and

threw a glance at Gladys, who seemed not to notice the sudden tension in the room. Then he gave me a look that touched a chord somewhere in my soul. "Entirely my pleasure, fair lady," he said softly.

This, I decided right then, was going to be the best Thanksgiving of my life.

The dinner turned out better than we'd hoped. Gladys's tea room seated twenty-four people comfortably, but so many people asked for reservations we managed to cram thirty in at each sitting.

We cooked four turkeys, thanks to Gladys's two oversize ovens. I was in charge of the vegetables and directed the two girls, while Gladys took care of the potatoes and gravy. The hams we served cold, peppered with cloves and pineapple slices. When I questioned that decision, Gladys told me she'd always served it that way, and seemed surprised when I told her I was used to baking ham in the oven.

Dan helped wait on the tables, and I could hear customers laughing at his comments. He was always trying to make people laugh, so no one would ever know how much he was hurting inside. The thought dampened my spirits, but I couldn't stay down for long. Everyone was having such a good time.

We all pitched in to wash dishes, which were needed for the second sitting, then had to be washed all over again.

"You need a dishwasher," I told Gladys as we dried and polished the wineglasses.

"I've got two." She waggled her hands at me. "They're right here."

"I meant a dishwashing machine." I picked up another wine glass and started polishing it. "It would save everyone so much time."

"Can't afford it." She waved a hand at the wall. "Besides, where would I put it?"

I had to admit there wasn't anywhere to put a dishwasher. "You'd have to remodel the kitchen, I guess."

"Gawd knows what that would cost."

"If you do many more dinners like this one, you could afford it. Invest in your business and it will grow. You could get a business loan from the bank."

She raised her eyebrows. "I could?"

"Sure. Judging by the sellout crowd we had today, the business is there. You just have to work out the most efficient way of running it."

"I could use a few tips on that subject," Dan said from behind me.

I hadn't noticed him come in and as usual my heart gave a little thump at his voice. "I'm not a business expert," I told him.

"Sounds as if you are. From what you told me, you ran your friend's health club."

I made a face at him. "I exaggerated."

"Business still slow, Dan?" Gladys gave him a look of pure sympathy.

He shrugged. "Practically nonexistent. Anyway, my lease is up next year. I'm thinking of looking for a job once winter's over. I hear they're looking for carpenters on the new building site in Chatswell."

I felt a pang of dismay. "Is that far?"

"Far enough. I'll probably look for a flat up there."

Gladys looked almost as stricken as I felt. "We'll miss you, luv."

"Yeah," Dan said, "I'll miss you, too." But he was looking at me as he said it.

"I should go out and see how Gillian's doing." I practically ran from the kitchen, reminding myself I had to stop reading meanings into his words that simply weren't there.

We'd pushed the tables together in the dining room, making two long tables, so that people could sit together and pass the food around, just like a family Thanksgiving.

The noise was deafening in that small room. Everyone kept raising their voices to be heard above their neighbors. Gillian sat at one end with Robbie next to her, and Ned sat on her right, keeping an eye on Sheila and Craig.

I reached them just in time to see Robbie tip his glass of apple juice across the table-cloth.

Gillian slapped his hand and he started to bawl at the top of his lungs. Ned said something to Gillian I couldn't hear, but judging from her expression it wasn't pleasant.

"He's probably tired," I said, as Gillian tried to hush the boy. "Let me take him for a bit. He can watch television in the living room until you're ready to go."

"Can I come?" Sheila asked eagerly.

Craig chimed in. "Me, too?"

Surprised he'd want to go anywhere with me, I answered him with a grin. "Sure! I'll show you how to play games on my computer."

Both Craig and Sheila scrambled off their chairs, and even Robbie stopped crying and held up his arms to me.

"We're ready to go now," Gillian said, giving Ned a dark look. "It's time the children were in bed."

Ned shoved his chair back and stood, while I smothered my protest. There was no point in arguing with Gillian, and in any case, I knew that almost everyone in the room watched us with avid interest. I didn't want to give them any more fuel for their gossip.

I had the uncomfortable feeling that many of the customers, if not all, knew our story, and waited to see how the two of us were handling the situation. If they expected a confrontation, they were due for a disappointment.

Gillian did thank me as they left. "It was the best dinner we've ever eaten," she said, as the children filed out into the street.

Warmed by her words, I had to stop myself from hugging her. "I'm glad you all enjoyed it," I said instead.

She uttered a bitter laugh. "Well, me and the kids enjoyed it. I can't say about Ned. You never know what he's thinking."

I watched her walk away, and I ached with sympathy. I knew what it was to live with a man for years without knowing who he really was inside. That lack of communication could mean disaster for a marriage.

I walked back into the tearoom, thinking that I already knew Dan better than I'd ever known my husband. It was a sobering thought.

As Christmas approached, Val's e-mails got further and further apart. Much as I loved the quiet of Miles End, I was beginning to pine for the frantic hustle and bustle that was Christmas in Seattle. I missed shopping in the big stores and browsing through the avalanche of catalogs that used to pile up in my mailbox every day.

I thought about driving to Stattenham to shop, then figured I'd have more of a choice if I shopped online. The gifts in the high street shops were nice, but the choice was poor and I wanted special gifts for my new family and friends.

Then I saw the clock sitting on Gillian's mantelpiece. I remembered then, where I'd seen it before.

It was also at Christmastime, about four or five years ago. I'd seen it in a catalog and had fallen in love with it. I'd pointed it out to Brandon, hoping he'd take the hint and buy it for me. Of course, he never did.

Coincidence, I told myself. There had to be thousands of those clocks in existence. Even so, it bothered me enough that I made up my mind to have a long chat with Gillian.

The first day of the grandkids' Christmas vacation, I offered to take Gillian into Stattenham to do some Christmas shopping. At first she gave me an argument.

"I can't leave the children alone," she told

me. "And Ned's got to work."

I could tell she would have liked the opportunity to shop in town, so I drove back to the tea shop and asked Gladys if she'd look after the kids until we got back. "You can play the games on the computer," I told her.

Having become a computer addict herself, she readily agreed and an hour later Gillian and I were on our way to Stattenham.

This was the first time Gillian and I had been alone outside of her house, and I felt edgy, to say the least. I asked questions about the kids, and received one- or two-word answers. After struggling to relieve the tension without much success, I decided to jump in with both feet.

"I saw a clock like the one on your mantelpiece while I was shopping online," I said. "It's a lovely little clock. Did you buy it in the village?"

I knew by the long pause that it wasn't a coincidence after all. "It was my mother's," Gillian said at last.

"I see." I sought for the right words to phrase my question. "You must miss her. How long has it been since she passed away?"

"Nearly four years."

I figured I had nothing to lose. "Brandon

sent it to her, didn't he?"

I felt her gaze on me. "How did you know?"

"I saw it in a catalog and pointed it out to him." I tried to keep the bitterness from my voice. "Of course, I had no idea he would buy it for your mother."

"I'm sorry."

The words were mumbled, and sounded just a little defensive, but they made me feel better, nonetheless. I decided to take advantage of her grudging sympathy.

"He must have kept in touch with your mother over the years. I'm sure he wanted to know all about you."

"No, he didn't. He didn't care about us at all." Her voice was low and fierce and I had to strain to catch the words in that strong accent of hers. "We never heard a word from him until he sent that clock. I don't know why he sent it. It made me mum cry."

That surprised me. I'd assumed he'd kept in touch with Eileen all these years. "He must have sent a letter with it."

"Yeah, he did that all right. Said he wanted her to know he'd never forgotten her." Her breath hissed out through her clenched teeth. "That's a laugh. Not a word for twenty-five years, then he sends her a bloody clock. He didn't even put his address on the letter."

I had an idea why Brandon had contacted Eileen again. I wondered if he'd known about his heart problem after all, and figured his time could be running out. Knowing Brandon, he would have refused surgery. He used to say that most operations were just an excuse for doctors to get more money out of people. This could have been his way of letting Eileen know before he died that she was still important to him.

Too bad he hadn't done the same for me.

"I was going to throw it out," Gillian muttered. "But it meant a lot to me mum. She kept it by her bed and she kept looking at it. She was looking at it when she died. I was there, but she didn't see me. All she saw was that bloody clock. I keep it on the mantelpiece to remind me of her."

And of her father, I thought, even though I knew she'd never admit it. My heart ached for her. I knew how it felt to watch other kids with their dads — the dreadful pain of loss and longing for what I couldn't have. Nothing in this world would ever fill that empty spot in her heart.

Right then I would have given anything to tell her that I shared her pain, but this just wasn't the time. Later, I promised myself,

when I was sure she'd understand. If that
time ever came.

CHAPTER 15

When we arrived in Stattenham, we spent a pleasant two hours drifting around the shops. Gillian didn't buy a lot, mostly small toys for the kids. I guessed she didn't have much money to spend. I planned on taking advantage of that.

I suggested we have lunch at The Cove, where I'd had dinner with Dan. Gillian seemed intimidated by the waiter, though she did her best not to show it. I guessed this was a new experience for her and did my best to put her at ease.

"Do you like fish?" I asked her as I scanned the menu. "I had the Dover sole the last time I was here. It's real good."

Her eyes widened. "You come all the way here to have lunch?"

"Dan Connelly gave me a ride when I came into town to rent my car. We had dinner here."

Her expression changed. "Oh, yeah. I

heard you went out with him."

I was tempted to tell her it wasn't a date, but decided against it. I didn't need to explain myself to anyone.

We both settled on the sole, and while we waited for our order I asked her about the kids.

She was a different person when she talked about her children. Animated, even laughing about something Robbie had told his teacher, she talked more to me then than she had in all the time I'd known her.

Encouraged by her relaxed attitude, I waited until we had our food in front of us before saying, "I regret so much not having children. I've missed out on so much."

Her face sobered at once. "It must have been hard."

"It was." I felt a stab of bitterness. I could forgive Brandon many things, I thought, except that. How I wish I knew why he'd lied to me. Maybe if I could understand why, I could forgive him that, too.

"I don't know what I'd do without my children." Gillian picked up her knife and fork. "They're all I've got now. Ned's no company these days. I hardly know he's there most of the time."

"Maybe he feels left out. You're so busy with your kids you really don't have much time together. Perhaps you could take a vacation together, just the two of you."

Her face turned stony. "Can't afford no holiday. Even if we could, Ned would never go away. We don't have much to say to each other these days."

I wanted to say so much. I wanted to tell her to talk to Ned, make him listen, demand he give her and the kids the attention they deserved.

It was too late for me, but there was still time for Gillian and Ned. She still cared about him. I'd seen it in her face so many times. Maybe, underneath all that indifference, Ned cared for his family, too. If only they would make the effort to reach out to each other, and really get to know each other, there was a chance they could make it work.

But I could say none of it. It wasn't what Gillian wanted to hear, especially from me, the other woman. Instead, I seized the opportunity to bring up my little plan.

"I thought, since we have a little time left this afternoon," I began, "that we might show your dolls' hats to a couple of buyers. It wouldn't hurt to see if there's any interest in selling them here."

Gillian's mouth tightened. "I don't have any left. I sold them all at the bazaar."

"Yes, I know. They flew off the stand. People just love them, and I know you could sell a lot of them in a town like this."

She dug a piece out of her fish and popped it into her mouth. I waited for her to stop chewing. "I can't sell what I don't have," she said finally.

"Well, as a matter of fact, I borrowed two of them from Sheila this morning. We could show them to the buyers, and take orders. It's too late for Christmas, anyway, which is a shame, but they might be interested in selling them to the summer visitors, and that will give you plenty of time to make some more."

I watched interest creep across her face, and pressed my point. "I'll help you with packaging and delivery, if you like. I'll even keep accounts for you. I can do it on the computer like I do Gladys's bookkeeping. It takes hardly any time at all."

Gillian poked at her food with her fork. "I don't know if they're good enough to sell in big-town shops."

"There's one way to find out. I went on-line and made a list of shops that might be interested. We'll just try a couple at first and see what happens. Okay?"

I held my breath while she took a mouthful of mashed potatoes and chewed it down.

"This is very good," she said, as she scooped peas onto her fork. "Almost as good as your Thanksgiving dinner."

That made me smile. "I'm glad you're enjoying it. Now, what about the hats?"

She shrugged. "All right, if you think it's worth a try."

I closed my fist under the table in triumph. I'd won another round. It was a hard battle, but as long as I was making headway, I'd keep on fighting until I'd broken through Gillian's tough resolve and won her friendship and respect. Even if I had to stay another three months to do it.

All five of the gift-shop buyers we visited seemed pleased to be offered Gillian's hats. "These are just so gorgeous," a young woman gushed. She held one of them up to the light to inspect it more closely. "I wish we could wear hats like these nowadays. So utterly feminine, don't you think?"

"I think they'd sell like hotcakes," I said, giving Gillian a nudge. I wanted her to conduct the business part of it, and so far I'd done all the talking in the previous shops. Gillian needed to handle this one.

She gave me a quick glance, then said nervously, "I'd be willing to sell them on consignment."

The woman clutched the hats to her chest

as if guarding them with her life. "How many can you deliver and how soon?"

Since we'd already promised a dozen to each of the previous shops I expected Gillian to offer the same amount. She seemed to think about it for a moment, then asked with more confidence, "How many would you like?"

The buyer studied the hats again. "I'll take fifty."

Gillian's jaw dropped, and I said quickly, "How about twenty-five by Easter and the rest a month later?"

The woman seemed disappointed. "All right. But I'd like to keep these two."

"I'm sorry." I held out my hand for the precious hats. "These two belong to my granddaughter, and we couldn't possibly let them go. Perhaps Mrs. Hodge can make you a couple and I'll bring them in later?"

Gillian turned to the buyer with one of her rare smiles. "I'll have them ready for you by next week."

Relieved, I followed her out of the shop and we walked to the car. "Well," I said, feeling pleased with myself, "I guess there's no doubt they think your hats will sell. I just hope I haven't piled too much work on you."

"I'll manage." She climbed into the car

next to me and I started the engine. "Thank you," she said. "I couldn't have done all that on my own."

"Yes, you could," I told her. "You just needed to know how, that's all."

She gave me a sidelong glance. "It's sort of exciting. Like I'm a real businesswoman."

"You are." I grinned at her. "Congratulations."

"I just hope I don't muck it up."

"You won't. You have a great product, and a steady stream of customers. Every doll in Stattenham and beyond will be wearing your hats."

She actually giggled.

Thrilled by the progress we'd made, I added, "I've learned a lot about the business taxes in England from Gladys. We'll have to keep account of what you spend on supplies, and other expenses, to offset the profits you make."

She sobered at once. "It all sounds so complicated."

"It's really not," I assured her. "In any case, I'll keep track of it all if you like. It's so easy to do with a computer."

She was silent for a while, probably going over everything in her mind. "I'd like to learn how to use a computer," she said at last. "Gladys says there's lots of exciting things you can learn with a computer. They have them at the school and my kids know how to use one."

"Then it's time you did, too." I pulled into a gas station, wincing as usual at the price of gas. It was three times what I paid for it in the States. "Whenever you have time I'll be happy to show you how to use mine."

I held my breath waiting for her answer.

"That'd be nice. Thanks."

"You're welcome." I smiled at her, and was rewarded with a quick smile back.

I drove home on a cloud of optimism. I'd achieved so much that day. I still had a ways to go before I felt that Gillian and I were truly friends, but I'd made an important breakthrough.

The day before Christmas Eve, Gladys left to spend the holidays with her daughter in London. She'd closed the tea shop until after New Year's Day. By the following night, all the shops in the high street would be closed until after New Year, leaving the whole place deserted.

Since our trip to Stattenham had been so successful, I'd hoped for an invitation to spend Christmas Day with the Hodges. When Christmas Eve day arrived without me hearing from her, I reluctantly made a reservation for Christmas dinner at the

White Stone Inn.

I tried not to feel sorry for myself, but thinking about all the activities at the health club, the dinner parties I'd attended with Brandon, the neighbors dropping by with cookies, the carol singers in the mall, I wanted to go back home so badly I was tempted to call the airlines and get the next flight out.

Instead I called Gillian and asked if I could drop off their Christmas presents. She invited me to stop by that afternoon and seemed pleased that I'd called.

I'd just finished talking to her when my cell phone pealed out its Christmas carol. Dan's voice greeted me with a bad imitation of Santa's hollow laugh.

"Ho, ho, ho to you, too," I answered, smiling.

"I just wanted to wish you a happy Christmas." He hesitated, then added, "I have something for you. If you're not doing anything this evening I thought I'd drop it by."

I glanced at the package sitting on my bed. I'd bought him a sweater. It had seemed a good idea at the time, but then I worried that I was going overboard and he might get the wrong impression. I'd decided to wait and see if he'd gotten anything for me before I gave it to him.

"No," I said, eager to reassure him. "I'm not doing anything. I'd love to see you. I have something for you, too."

"Oh, good. I love presents."

Again I waited through a short pause.

"I thought you might be going over to Gillian's," he said finally. "Gladys told me you two are starting up a business venture together."

I laughed. "Not really. Gillian is selling some of her sewing projects in gift shops in Stattenham. I offered to help her with the book work, that's all. I'm seeing her this afternoon, but I'm free for this evening."

"Okay. How about dinner at the Unicorn?"

"On the condition I pay."

His sigh echoed down the line. "How many times do I have to tell you — I invite, I pay."

"Then let me pay half."

"Persistent, aren't you."

"We Yanks tend to be bullheaded."

"I'd never have guessed. Sorry, love, but I'm paying. End of argument."

I had gotten used to being called "love" by the locals, much as Val called everyone "hon," back home. Somehow, when Dan said it, the term seemed more personal.

"I suppose you'll be going over to Gillian's house for Christmas dinner, then?" Dan asked, when I didn't answer.

"As a matter of fact, I haven't been invited." I paused, feeling my way. "What are you doing about Christmas dinner?"

"I usually eat it at the pub. I get offers every year, but I have an idea people feel sorry for me and feel obligated to invite me, so I usually turn them down."

I stared at the carefully wrapped package on my bed. Maybe I was going out on a limb, but it was Christmas, when all things were possible. "I owe you a couple of dinners," I said, doing my best to sound casual. "How about I come over there and cook for you?" I was sure he could hear my heart pounding as I waited for his reply.

He sounded wary when he answered me. "Roast beef? Yorkshire pudding?"

I swallowed. "I'm more used to cooking turkey, but I can make roast beef. The Yorkshire pudding is a bit beyond my expertise, I'm afraid."

"Don't worry, I have a recipe. We'll muddle through."

I glanced at my watch. "I'd better shop before they all close."

"No, you go and see Gillian. I'll get whatever we need. You like Christmas pudding? Rum sauce? Mince pies?"

I wasn't sure how my waistline was going to stand up to all those puddings, but it was worth the risk. "Whatever you can find. It's a bit late to be shopping for Christmas dinner."

"Pray do not worry, fair lady. I hereby promise you a veritable feast, by George."

I was still laughing when I closed the phone. Suddenly my bleak Christmas had turned into a warm, exciting, meaningful celebration. I barely remembered to call the inn and cancel my reservation.

Craig answered the door to my knock that afternoon. His eyes widened as I piled a bulging red plastic bag into his arms. Sheila and Robbie danced up and down behind him in excitement, until Gillian's voice pulled them back into the room.

The house smelled the way houses should at Christmas — a hint of pine, spices and something sweet baking in the oven. Gillian hurried toward me and took the other bag from my arms. "This is so kind of you," she said, a little too formally for my liking. "And much too generous."

"Oh, I had fun." I meant it. It was the first time I'd shopped for kids and only my limited bank account kept me from spoiling them outrageously.

"We don't open up presents until Christmas morning," Gillian said, as she piled the gifts under a small tree. "Goodness, you did buy a lot."

"They're only small things," I assured her. "I figured quantity would be more fun than quality."

I'm not sure she understood what I meant but her smile was enough for me. "Sheila," she ordered. "Give Mrs. Maitland the presents we got for her."

That took the edge off my enjoyment. Although the kids had been calling me Nana for some time, Gillian still couldn't bring herself to call me anything but Mrs. Maitland. Time, I promised myself. Once we got into the business of selling the hats maybe Gillian would ease up. With that thought in mind I concentrated on what the kids were telling me about their school concerts.

Ned came in just as I was about to leave. It was already dark, which was something else I found hard to accept. By four in the afternoon the daylight faded to dusk, which made for a very long night.

"It's trying to snow," Ned said gruffly, with a nod in my direction.

The kids squealed and shouted in unison. "Can we get the sled out?" Craig asked, his face alight with hope.

"It's not settling yet." Ned disappeared up the stairs, leaving three disappointed faces behind.

"Does it snow much here?" I asked Gillian.

"Not much." She busied herself picking up empty teacups from the coffee table. "Hardly ever at Christmas. Most years we don't get any at all. Not like up north. They get a lot."

"Wished we lived up north," Craig grumbled.

"No you don't. You wouldn't get the nice summers we get here." Gillian gave him a sharp look. "Did you clean up your bedroom like I told you to?"

Craig scowled. "It's not my turn. Sheila's supposed to do it."

"Uh-uh!" Sheila shook her head so hard her pigtails whipped her face. "Not my turn, so there." She stuck her tongue out at her brother.

"You both go do it," Gillian ordered. "Or Father Christmas won't come tonight."

"There isn't —" Craig started to say, then snapped his mouth shut when his mother raised her hand.

"What did I tell you?"

Craig muttered something under his

breath, then went out into the hallway and dragged himself up the stairs. Sheila shot one look at Gillian and followed him.

"They get excited," Gillian said, ignoring Robbie, who was tugging at her skirt. "Sometimes they forget their manners."

"They are extremely well behaved kids." I patted Robbie on the head and basked in the smile he gave me. "You're doing a great job with them."

Her cheeks turned pink. "Thank you. I do my best."

I glanced at the little clock that Brandon had sent all the way from Seattle to a woman he'd never forgotten. "I'd better be going. I have a date tonight."

I'd said it without thinking. I saw Gillian's eyes widen. She turned away, then bent down to pick up a stray silver icicle that had fallen from the tree.

I felt embarrassed, though I wasn't sure why. "Actually, it's not really a date. It's just . . . you know . . . dinner."

She straightened, though she wouldn't look at me. "Talking about dinner, I was wondering if you'd like to come over for Christmas dinner tomorrow. The kids would like it and they could thank you properly for their presents."

I was thrilled that she'd finally asked me,

but now I was in a difficult position. Dan was already shopping for groceries. I could hardly tell him I'd changed my mind. "I'm sorry," I said, and hoped she knew how truly sorry I was, "but I've already made plans for dinner tomorrow."

She looked surprised, then her expression changed and I knew she'd figured it out. "That's okay. Another time."

"I'd love that. Really."

She nodded. "Well, thank you for the presents."

"Merry Christmas, Gillian." I wanted so much to hug her, but I knew that would be overstepping the boundaries she'd set.

She called up the stairs to Sheila and Craig, and they came tumbling down. Each one of the kids gave me a hug and a kiss on the cheek. Robbie clung a little longer, and I rubbed my cheek against his silky head.

I loved all three of my grandkids, but this little guy was my favorite. Right then I felt a surge of tenderness that brought tears to my eyes. Reluctantly, I let him go, wished them all a merry Christmas and left.

One part of me wanted so much to be with them on Christmas Day. My family. It was a dream come true for me. But a more urgent part of me wanted to be with Dan.

After all, there would be other Christmases, and Seattle was only nine hours away. I'd already promised myself that I would come back as often as I could afford. I had no intention of losing touch with my family now that I had one.

But this would be the only Christmas I'd ever spend with Dan. By the spring he'd have left town, and no matter how many times I came back, it was unlikely I'd ever see him again.

Oh, yes, I knew it was stupid of me. I was chasing rainbows, and there'd be no pot of gold at the end of this one. But one day. Just one day of knowing the intense, heady excitement of being with someone who could make me feel like a real woman again. At my age that was earth-shattering, and I looked forward to it with all the eagerness and anticipation of a teenager.

CHAPTER 16

While I was in Stattenham with Gillian I'd bought a royal-blue dress in a soft wool. It was a little more feminine than I was used to wearing, with a deep V front and a slightly flared skirt that just brushed my knees.

I admit, I'd had Dan in mind when I'd tried it on, and when Gillian said she liked it, that had settled the matter.

I wore that dress on Christmas Eve for my dinner with Dan. The crowd inside the pub sounded much more rowdy than our first visit, and conversation was difficult.

At least, I told myself that was the reason. The truth was, I was on edge, jittery with anticipation of being alone with Dan in his home. He seemed nervous as well, and his gaze kept skidding away from me as if he were reluctant to meet my eyes.

I tried to ease the tension by telling him about Christmas in Seattle. "The best part,"

I told him, "is buying the Christmas tree. I'm lucky enough to live in the Northwest, where most of them grow, so we could get a really big one for a reasonable amount. Douglas fir, ponderosa pine, we get all sorts to choose from. My favorite is the blue spruce, but Brandon always picked out a Scotch pine. I don't like all those spaces between the branches. Though I guess it's easier to hang stuff on them."

His expression was comical. "I have absolutely no idea what you're talking about."

Covered with confusion, I stumbled over my answer. "You don't? But you have Christmas trees. I've seen them in the town square."

"As far as I know, we only have one kind. A Christmas tree. That's it. I wouldn't know a blue spruce from a Scotch pine if my life depended on it."

"Oh. Well, the blue spruce has thick needles and they're sort of cushiony and it's a beautiful blue-green color, and . . ." I broke off. "You're laughing at me."

"I'm not laughing, I'm smiling." His eyes crinkled at the edges. "You really enjoy Christmas, don't you."

"Yes, I do." It must have been the wine, as I added, "Especially this one."

Our eyes met, and above all that loud

chatter and laughter, a silent message seemed to pass between us. Dan's smile faded, and the look on his face disturbed me, though I couldn't have said why.

I tried to keep up the joking comments after that, but everything I said seemed to fall flat, and by the time he paid the bill, I was miserably certain he regretted accepting my suggestion to spend Christmas Day together.

Snowflakes drifted down as we walked to his car, and all around us people laughed, hugged and called out greetings. Lights twinkled around the quaint windows of the pub, and splashed color on the white dusting of snow at our feet.

I waited until we were settled in the car before asking, "What do I owe you for the groceries?"

He started the engine, then gave me a quizzical look. "You're not going to start that again, are you?"

"This is supposed to be my payback dinner," I reminded him. "There's not much point if you buy the groceries."

"You'll be doing most of the work. That's enough payback for me. I haven't had a home-cooked Christmas dinner in years."

"For all you know I'm a lousy cook and

you'll end up wishing you had dinner at the pub."

"Nah. I have every confidence in you."

I felt a twinge of apprehension. "I hope I live up to your expectations."

"You've already done that. I sampled your cooking at your American Thanksgiving dinner, remember?"

"Actually Gladys did most of it."

He glanced over his shoulder as he reversed out of the parking spot. "You worry too much. Just relax. It'll be fun."

That made me feel better, and we chatted more easily as he drove me back to the tea shop.

"What time do you want me over tomorrow?" I asked, as I got ready to hop out of the car.

"How early do you get up?"

I couldn't quite see his expression in the shadows, but I knew he was serious. "I'm usually up about eight."

"Well, Christmas Day starts with opening gifts and then breakfast. We might as well make a day of it."

I smiled. "Ten o'clock too early?"

"I'll have the kettle on."

"See you tomorrow then." I reached for the handle and was surprised when he climbed out and came around to help me out of the car.

"Watch your step," he warned. "There's not much snow but it could be slippery."

I let him take my arm and stepped out into the cold. "Thanks. Is there anything I can bring tomorrow?"

I expected him to let go of me, but he held on. "Just yourself."

"Okay, then. Thanks for dinner. I really enjoyed it."

"Did you?"

I could see his face now, reflected in the streetlamp. He looked worried. "Yes," I said softly. "I did. Very much."

He stood there, looking down at me, his fingers gripping my arm. "Me, too." He looked away, lifted his chin as if coming to a decision, then looked back at me. "You looked very nice tonight. Quite lovely, in fact."

My throat was too tight to answer him. No one had ever called me lovely before. I tried to imagine what it was he saw, but all I could envision was a middle-aged lady with a few gray hairs and not much of a waistline.

True, he had a few wrinkles. Especially around his eyes and at the corners of his mouth. His hair was white at the temples, and beginning to recede from his forehead.

But looking at him in the softening glow of the streetlamp, with the snowflakes drifting down and clinging to the shoulders of his dark gray coat, I thought he was the most handsome guy to ever walk the earth.

I sent up a silent prayer. *Thank you, God.*

Aloud I murmured, "Thank you, sir. You are most kind."

"Not at all, my fair lady." Taking me completely by surprise, he leaned forward and dropped a light kiss on my frozen mouth. "See you tomorrow."

His lady. Oh, if only I were. Before I could respond, he took off around the hood of the car and jumped in. I watched him drive off, knowing without a doubt that as long as I lived, I would never again feel quite the way I felt that Christmas Eve, standing on the empty street in the tiny village of Miles End.

By the time I woke up the next morning, I'd bounced back to reality. It was the Christmas season, after all, when everyone got a little emotional. If I had any sense at all, I'd forget what happened last night, and stop putting too much meaning into what was, after all, little more than a simple display of friendship.

Even so, it took me much longer than usual to get ready for my day. First I had to open my gifts from the Hodges. Sitting alone in my comfortable little room, a cup of steaming coffee at my elbow, I unwrapped a gorgeous fluffy wool scarf in my favorite shades of blue and amethyst. Gillian had done her homework, and I was touched by the thought she'd put into the gift.

The package from the grandkids turned out to be a bright red umbrella that telescoped down to a quarter its size to fit into a neat little case. I also opened my gift from Val. She'd sent me my favorite body lotion, which I hadn't been able to find in Stattenham, and a calendar of Washington State that immediately gave me pangs of homesickness.

After that I scrambled to get dressed. In my haste I dropped the cap from the toothpaste, and had to hunt for it under the dresser. Then I broke a nail and spent way too long filing all my nails to the same length.

I couldn't decide what to wear and changed three times before I decided on black slacks and a red sweater. I lost my car keys and finally found them in the pocket of the jacket I'd worn the night before.

It was already ten past ten when I let myself out of the tea shop and walked down the road to the garage. It took all my willpower not to gun the engine as I drove up the hill and past the Merry Unicorn.

The small amount of snow that had fallen the day before had melted and the pavement had dried out. A weak sun was trying to peek through the billowy white clouds drifting across the sky. The boats in the harbor hardly rocked at all, though a mist hid the view of the shoreline from the top of the hill.

There's always something special about a frosty Christmas morning, and this one in particular filled me with a delicious anticipation that was hard to resist. I was looking forward to being alone with Dan for the whole day with all the excitement of a six-year-old awaiting Santa.

At the same time, I couldn't quite dismiss a niggling worry. I guess I was afraid that the longer I was with him, the harder it would be to ignore my growing attachment to him. I only hoped I could hide my emotions. I was sure he'd be appalled if he knew how I really felt.

That gave me a jolt. Until that moment, I hadn't analyzed my true feelings. I was reluctant to admit I was already far too fond of the man.

I arrived twenty minutes late. Dan greeted me with his usual enthusiasm, and led me up the stairs to his apartment. Though somewhat masculine with its brown leather armchairs, paneled walls and uncluttered bookshelves, the living room was clean and tidy.

Gas flames licked at artificial logs in the fireplace, and a fluffy oval rug helped make the whole room cozy. The only Christmas decorations I could see were miniature snowmen marching across the mantelpiece among sprigs of holly, and a Santa, complete with eight reindeer, swooping across the living-room window in his sleigh. All, I suspected, hastily bought along with the groceries yesterday.

Warmed by the effort he'd put into the day, I accepted the package he gave me and handed him the sweater. I'd spent practically every waking hour since his call the day before trying to guess what he might have bought me. I was utterly charmed when I opened the package and found three horse brasses mounted on a wide strip of red leather.

I was so busy inspecting them I didn't see him open his package, but I heard his murmur of pleasure. I looked up to see him holding the sweater against his chest.

"I hope it fits," I said, my heart racing at his expression when he looked at me.

"This is brilliant." He held it away from

him to examine it. "Great color."

I'd chosen pale blue, since most of the clothes I'd seen him in were dark gray and black. I watched him pull it on over his golf shirt and zip it up. "That should keep you warm," I said lightly, even though my throat was tight just watching the pleasure on his face.

"Warm as toast. Thanks so much. It's a terrific present."

He had that look in his eyes again and I had to turn away. Muttering "you're welcome," I studied the brasses in my hand. One of them had a lighthouse on it, another a castle and the third had a unicorn. "These are absolutely beautiful. Thank you. I'll treasure them forever." I could hear the slight tremble in my voice, and hoped he couldn't.

"I thought they'd remind you of your visit here. You've seen the castle and had dinner at the Unicorn. I hope you'll have time to let me show you the lighthouse before you go back home."

Home. I'd been so homesick the past few days, yet now the word seemed confusing to me. I felt disoriented, as if I were floating between two worlds, without belonging to either one.

I wasn't sure I wanted to go home, but

the thought of never going back was inconceivable. Much as I loved this little village and the people in it, I didn't belong here. I belonged in Seattle. Didn't I?

I pushed the unsettling thoughts away. I'd worry about that later. All I wanted now was to enjoy these few hours I'd been granted. I looked up, my heart floundering as I looked at Dan's smiling face. "I'd love to see the lighthouse. I hear it's haunted."

"It's supposed to be, but I haven't seen any ghosts. Maybe they'll come out for you."

"I'd rather they didn't."

He laughed, and the fragile web of intimacy was broken. "How about breakfast? Scrambled eggs, sausage and bacon? Not exactly gourmet, but it will keep us going until dinner."

All at once I was ravenous. "It sounds wonderful. I haven't had a cooked breakfast since I left the inn. Gladys's pastries are so delicious, I've been eating one every single morning."

"Right then." He nodded his head at the television set across the room. "I don't know that there's much to watch on TV but —"

I interrupted him. "No, I want to help you."

He smiled. "I never turn down an offer like that."

I followed him into his neat and sparkling kitchen. The lack of counter space would have driven me crazy, but a small table in the corner provided some room to work. As with most things I'd encountered in this enchanting country, the appliances reminded me of children's toys. They weren't a whole lot bigger.

At five feet, five inches, I was a little taller than the fridge. The freezer was on the bottom, which would involve a lot of bending. A good way to get my waistline back in shape.

We cooked what seemed an enormous amount of food for the two of us. Scrambled eggs, sausages, fried potatoes, fried tomatoes, fried mushrooms — Dan even fried the bread. I tried not to think about all that cholesterol and cleaned my plate. I couldn't remember when breakfast had ever tasted that good.

After we'd washed dishes — by hand, since Dan didn't have a dishwasher — we sat with a cup of coffee at the little table in the kitchen. Our knees kept bumping, and I had trouble concentrating on what Dan was telling me.

"We have to listen to the queen's speech." He looked at his watch. "In about half an hour."

I'd been watching news about the royal family for weeks, thoroughly captivated by all the pomp and circumstance surrounding them. "Really? What's the speech about?"

"Every Christmas Day the queen gives a chat to the nation. She talks about what's happened in the country the past year and tells us some of her plans for the future."

"Oh. Kind of like our State of the Union address."

"Yeah, I suppose. Anyway, it's a tradition. Everyone tunes in to watch, toasts the queen when it's over, then talks about what she said for a week afterward."

"Sounds familiar. Except for the toasting part, and we talk about the state of the union for a day then forget it."

He grinned. "That fascinating, huh?"

I made a face. "I try not to pay much attention to politics. Unless I'm voting, then I read through every bit of information on the issues, terrified I'll do something wrong and vote for something I'm absolutely against."

"Of course." He nodded, his face solemn. "I mean, if you didn't cast the right vote the whole country would collapse, right?"

I sighed. "I know. I worry too much."

"That you do." He got up from the table. "Come on, bring your coffee and we'll watch the queen before we tackle dinner."

All this "we" stuff was beginning to sound incredibly personal. It was also comfortable and relaxing. I was amazed how at ease I felt, as if I'd known Dan for years.

We settled in front of the television, warmed by the fire and a homey together-ness that had been no more than the stuff of my dreams until now. The queen's speech was entertaining, not only in content, but in the impeccable way she delivered it.

We sat and discussed the speech afterward, ending in a spirited yet friendly argument about the immigration laws and the impact they had on our respective countries. The thought occurred to me that if I decided to stay in England, I'd be an immigrant myself.

Unnerved that I was actually considering such a drastic move, I commented on the time, and the fact that vegetables awaited us in the kitchen.

I really don't know how we got dinner cooked that afternoon.

We'd saluted the queen with a glass of cream sherry, which Dan assured me was the proper drink for a toast. He'd followed that by opening a bottle of wonderful French wine, and things deteriorated from there.

After poring over a recipe, I mixed up the

batter for the Yorkshire pudding, but must have done something wrong as the moment I took it out of the oven it collapsed like a punctured tire.

Dan forgot to add water to the vegetables, and singed the bottom of the saucepan. I scraped the worst of the black off, added butter and brown sugar and told him they were now American glazed carrots.

The beef turned out great, though a little overdone for my taste, and the brandy-soaked plum pudding was an instant hit. We played tug-of-war with Christmas crackers — brightly wrapped paper tubes that snapped apart to spill out miniature trinkets — and for the rest of the meal we wore the silly paper hats we'd found inside.

Sitting across from each other by the fire, we finished what was left of the brandy and ignored the dishes piled high in the sink.

"You know what's missing?" Dan murmured, as we listened to Christmas music playing quietly in the background.

"I can't think of a single thing." I waved my glass at him, my vision just slightly blurred by all the alcohol I'd consumed. "Everything is absolutely perfect."

He treated me to his infectious grin again. "You're so easy to please."

"Thank you." I leaned back in my chair

with a happy sigh. "That was such a wonderful dinner."

"Best ever. You did yourself proud."

"I couldn't have done it without you."

He took another sip of his brandy. "We make a good team."

"A great team." I was feeling sleepy, and barely managed to stifle a yawn. "I always did like the idea of a man who could cook."

"If you can call it cooking. Usually I open a frozen dinner and heat it up in the microwave."

I peered at him through my haze of well-being. "It must be hard for a man to take care of himself."

"You get used to it." He put his glass down on the table in front of him. "But back to what's missing." He stood up, and something about his expression made my spine tingle. "I know what it is."

I sat up, clenching the arms of the chair. "What is it?"

"Mistletoe."

All the strength flowed out of my legs. "Mistletoe?"

I'd squeaked the word but he didn't seem to notice. "Mistletoe." He moved over to the fireplace. "Nope, don't have any. This will have to do." He plucked a sprig of holly from underneath one of the snowmen.

It fell over, sending the rest of them top-pling. One dropped to the floor and rolled across the tiled fireplace. I kept my gaze glued to it as Dan took a couple of steps toward me.

"Okay, Marge," he said, bending over me. "Imagine this is mistletoe and pucker up."

I don't know if it was the brandy, or nerves, or maybe both.

I did the unforgivable.

I giggled.

CHAPTER 17

The giggle turned into a spurt of laughter that I tried desperately to control. I couldn't look at Dan's face. I felt terrible that I'd spoiled his big moment, but it wasn't exactly the romantic overture I'd been secretly hoping for all day. My imagination had supplied plenty of scenarios. None of them came close to this.

I expected a frozen silence, or an embarrassed attempt at brushing off the incident. What I didn't expect was the answering belly laugh that exploded above my head.

We laughed ourselves silly, until I managed between gasps, "I'm sorry. It just sounded so funny. . . ."

He pulled me out of the chair, still laughing. And then we weren't laughing anymore.

We kissed like two lovers who had gone far too long without seeing each other. We kissed as if we were afraid that any minute we'd be torn apart never to be together again. We kissed as though it were our last day on earth, and all the time in the world was running out.

Which, of course, it was.

The warning clanged in my head and sent a cold stream of reality down my back. I pulled away from Dan, struggling to regain my breath and my sanity.

"The dishes," I said, waving a hand toward the kitchen. "We've got to do the dishes."

"The dishes can wait." He reached for me again, but I backed away from him.

"No, they can't. They'll be much harder to wash if we leave them any longer."

He looked confused, shook his head, then said in a strange, flat voice, "Okay, we'll do the dishes if you insist."

I hurried to the kitchen, misery swallowing me up in a huge black cloud. I kept talking while I ran hot water over the mess in the sink. I talked about the health club, telling him silly things about Val and some of the weird customers who sometimes wandered in.

He nodded and smiled, but the light had gone out of his face. Instead of his usual comments, all I got was an occasional "Uh-huh."

I wanted to cry, and knew I couldn't. I wanted to throw down the dishcloth and throw myself into his arms. Those brief moments I'd spent there I knew would burn in my memory for as long as I lived.

Maybe I was a fool. Maybe any other woman would have taken whatever he'd offered and gone along for the ride. Val surely would have done.

But I wasn't Val. I was afraid of being hurt. I didn't have the courage to risk being left alone again to pick up the shattered pieces. It would much easier to leave him if I kept our relationship on a casual basis. Tough as it would be, I had to stick with that. It was time I did what was best for me, instead of trying to be what someone else wanted me to be.

Somehow we got through the rest of that evening. I left early, numbed by the strained conversation and the detached look on Dan's face.

"I'll give you a ring," he said, as he walked me to the car. "We'll set up a time to see the lighthouse."

I nodded, too wrapped up in my own misery to answer.

"That's if you still want to go with me."

I heard the question in his voice and found my tongue. "Of course I want to go. It will be fun." I knew my tone didn't match my words, and he barely smiled as he opened the car door for me to climb in.

He waited until I had the engine running, then leaned in the door so I could hear him. "I'm sorry. I was an idiot. Put it down to a little too much of the Christmas spirits."

Even then he could joke. I managed a smile. "There's no need to apologize. I had a good time. Really. It was a lovely Christmas."

"Yeah." He straightened. "Drive carefully."

My tight throat prevented me from forming words. I nodded, slipped the gear into Drive and pulled away from him. The last I saw of his reflection in the rearview mirror, he was standing in the middle of the road, staring after me.

The next day I decided to call Val and thank her for her gift. I felt it would be more personal, and although I didn't want to admit as much, I really needed to hear her voice. She asked her usual loaded questions and I answered them as best I could.

I filled her in on the latest news about Gillian and avoided a lengthy exchange about Dan. I did admit I'd spent Christmas Day with him, but managed to make it sound fairly impersonal, much to Val's disappointment.

"So when are you coming home?" she

demanded, when we'd finally caught up on everything.

"I haven't really decided." I knew I should make a decision soon. The rent Gillian paid me barely kept me in food and my share of the utilities. I had already dipped into my bank account for Christmas, and I couldn't go on doing that for much longer. I'd need money for two months' rent and a security deposit when I got back to the States, and enough to hold me over until I found a job.

As if reading my mind, Val said, "I could really use you at the club. At least until you get a job with the schools. I'm muddling along on my own right now. The last two idiots I hired didn't work out."

"What about the woman you hired to replace me?"

"Angela? Oh, she decided to open up a place of her own. That's the thanks I get from her after everything I taught her. Now she's trying to be my freaking competition. Can you believe that?"

"I'm sorry, Val."

"Me, too. I hate bookkeeping. So hurry home and take care of it for me, okay?"

"I'll let you know," I promised.

After I hung up I called Gillian to thank her for the gifts. To my utter surprise she invited me over that afternoon for Boxing

Day dinner. I'd forgotten that it was part of the Christmas holiday, and I eagerly accepted. That was exactly what I needed, to be with my family.

In spite of a twinge of heartache whenever Christmas Day was mentioned, I enjoyed my visit with the grandkids. We played with their new toys, watched television together and Robbie sang his version of "Away in a Manger" for me. He had the words muddled and sang instead, "The cattle are blowing the baby away," and I had to smother a laugh.

Gillian and I discussed her plans for her doll's hat business, and even Ned managed a little more than his customary sentence about the weather. It was a pleasant, relaxing afternoon, and it was with genuine regret that I left my little family to go home to my cold, lonely room.

Dan called later that week as I was working on the year end accounts for Gladys. "I was wondering if you had plans for New Year's Eve," he said, while I was still trying to deal with hearing his voice on the phone. "The Unicorn always puts on a good bash. I thought you might like to come along."

I couldn't think of anything I'd like more. I remembered reading somewhere the myth that whatever you are doing when the New

Year is born you'll be doing for the rest of that year.

There was no way that could be true for me.

Every fiber of my being wanted to be with him on what was one of the most romantic nights of the year. For that very reason I made a painful decision. "I'm sorry, but I promised the grandkids I'd see the New Year in with them." I hoped Gillian would agree to that when I suggested it, and not make a liar out of me. "I didn't spend Christmas with them," I added for good measure, "so I promised them New Year's."

"Okay. Just thought I'd ask."

Long after he hung up I sat there with my phone in my hand, wondering how something that was supposed to be in my best interests could hurt so damn much.

Gillian agreed to my spending New Year's Eve with them, and although the kids fell asleep and had to be carried to bed by ten-thirty, Gillian, Ned and I toasted the New Year in with the bottle of cream sherry I'd taken over there.

Gillian got a little giggly, and even Ned must have been mellowed by the alcohol. He lifted his glass and said in his gruff voice, "Here's to my wife's new business. Hope it's successful." He took a gulp of the sherry, then added, "I'm proud of you, girl."

The look of surprised pleasure on Gillian's face made me want to hug him.

I felt very satisfied with myself as I drove back to the tea shop. I'd pretty much accomplished what I'd set out to do. Not only was Gillian letting down her guard, things seemed to be improving with Ned, now that they had something tangible to talk about.

I still didn't have the answers I wanted as to why Brandon had married me instead of Eileen, why he had lied about being sterile, or why he had left the cottage to me instead of to Gillian. Maybe I never would. Maybe the answers weren't as important as I'd first thought.

Lying in bed later, I wondered how Dan had spent the evening, and tried not to imagine how we would have celebrated the New Year. I kept remembering that moment in his living room, and the heat in our kissing. How much I wanted to listen to my heart and the deep yearnings of my body instead of the warning voices in my head.

Had we been together tonight, I might have silenced those voices. And lived to regret it in the cold light of day. I fell asleep hugging my pillow, imagining it was Dan's warm body I held in my arms.

Gladys arrived home complaining bitterly

about the awful week she'd had with her daughter and grandsons. Apparently the thirteen-year-old-twins had shaken the house with their rock music, had kept Gladys awake by watching TV late at night, and generally behaved like normal, rowdy teenagers caught up in Christmas excitement.

The days passed without my realizing it. I spent most of them working out expansion plans with Gladys, who seemed excited about the prospect of enlarging the tea shop. I also spent some time with Gillian, and even managed to persuade her to let me take the kids on a drive now and then. She was always too busy with her hat project to go, but she seemed happy enough to have the kids off her hands for a while.

She didn't call me Mrs. Maitland anymore. She called me Nana when the kids were around and when they weren't she avoided calling me anything. I was impressed when she told me Ned had made her a sewing chest to store all her fabrics and sewing notions. He was actually taking an interest in her business venture. I couldn't be more happy for her.

Dan and I slipped back into our kidding around, and it was as if Christmas had never happened. Now and again I'd remember, and feel an aching sadness for what might have been, but then Dan would make me laugh with one of his silly jokes and the moment passed.

We shared lunch now and then, and went back to the Unicorn to celebrate Dan's birthday. Once in a while I'd catch him looking at me in a speculative way, as if trying to figure out what I was thinking. We both avoided personal comments, and I missed that part of our relationship, but there was less tension between us now, and that was a good thing.

I kept putting off making a decision to leave, and it was almost the end of January when Dan called me to ask if I wanted to see the lighthouse. I'd been waiting for him to say something, and had been tempted a couple of times to suggest it myself, so I jumped at the offer.

We set off that afternoon, and drove up the coastline to the lighthouse. Perched on a soaring cliff jutting out to sea, the gray stone tower and scalloped edging around the lantern reminded me a little of the castle.

The lighthouse keeper's cottage was roomy and smelled of raw fish. Pictures hung on the walls of previous keepers of the light, some of them dating back over two centuries.

The guard told us some scary tales about ghosts then led us through a door and invited us to climb the stairs to the top. There seemed to be an awful lot of them, and I worried that my legs might not carry me up all of them.

I wasn't about to admit that much to Dan, however. I let him go first, determined I'd keep up if it killed me. The jacket I wore was no match for the damp chill inside the tower, and I could feel the goose bumps rising on my arms. Maybe all those ghost stories had something to do with that.

The steps were wide on one side and narrow on the other, and I had to concentrate on where to put my feet. Twice I bumped into Dan when he paused for breath, and I wasn't sure if it was the climb warming my body or the contact with his.

As we neared the top, my legs began trembling and I paused for a break. "I don't know if I can make it any farther," I said, my words coming out in little jerks as I fought for breath.

"Of course you can." He was breathing hard, too. "You've come this far. You've got to get to the top now. I promise, the view will be worth it."

Considering there was a thick mist hugging the beach all the way from the village,

I seriously doubted that. Not to be outdone, however, I waved a weak hand at him. "Okay, let's go. But don't be surprised if you have to carry me down."

"Be a lot easier than carrying you up."

I wrinkled my nose at his retreating back and trudged up the remaining stairs close behind him.

At last he reached the platform, and turned to wait for me. It was at that moment that my legs finally gave out. I stumbled, and pitched forward.

Dan moved fast, and caught me under the arms. He dragged me back onto my feet and held me close to his body while I struggled to get air back into my lungs.

"Sorry," I said, panting like a tired bloodhound. "Guess I'm not as young as I used to be."

"Who is?" He smiled down at me, and I was suddenly very conscious of how close we were.

If I could have stepped backward I would have, but there was nothing behind me but the stairs, and I knew my legs would buckle again if I tried to step down.

Desperate to lighten the moment, I attempted a weak joke. "Do you think they'd mind if I took up residence here? I don't think I can make it down again."

"Sure you can. You can do anything you want if you put your mind to it."

I had the feeling he was trying to tell me something, but I wasn't sure what it was. I could feel my pulse racing, and knew we were approaching a dangerous line again. I had to step back and hope my legs would hold up.

I placed my hands gently against his chest and said lightly, "Thanks. I feel better now. I think I can actually stand up on my own."

Instead of moving away as I'd hoped, he stayed where he was and took hold of my hands, imprisoning them against his chest. I remember thinking how warm was his grasp, and how cold my fingers must feel in his.

"Marjorie," he said, so softly I could barely make out the words. "Why do you keep pushing me away? What are you so afraid of?"

Confused, I tried to pull my hands from his, but he wouldn't let go. "I'm not pushing you away," I said. "I'm just trying to avoid complications."

He looked at me for a long moment, and for a second I saw the same anguish in his eyes that I'd seen that first night in the Unicorn. Then he dropped my hands and turned toward the little glass door behind him.

He walked through it, and waited for me to follow him. My heart pounding with anxiety, I stepped inside a world of glass.

I shall never forget my first view from the top of that lighthouse. The mist had thinned out, and although the beach still looked hazy, I could see all along the coastline to the village of Miles End.

Following Dan around the massive lantern, I saw miles of ocean, gray and heaving beneath an endless sky. On the other side the jagged cliffs rose and fell until they disappeared in the mist far to the north of us.

A little farther on I saw the Devon moors sweeping down to a maze of small fields. They were separated by stone walls, tiny trees and white fences. I spotted a train snaking along the edge of the fields and felt as if I were looking at a miniature railroad, where I could just stretch out my hand and pluck one of those little trees from its stand.

Dan hadn't said a word since we'd stepped inside this mystic glass paradise, and I glanced at him. Hoping he'd forgotten the little incident outside, I murmured, "What an incredible view. It's breathtaking."

He nodded, though he wouldn't look at

me. "I knew you'd like it."

I felt compelled to say something, anything to take that look off his face. "Dan, I'm sorry. I didn't mean to upset you. I love being with you, I really do. You've made this visit very special for me. But I'll be leaving soon and —"

"Why?"

The sharp question took me by surprise. "Why? Because I have to go home."

He looked at me then, and I could see he was angry. Somehow I knew that whatever was said in the next few minutes between us would decide our relationship one way or another, and I was deathly afraid I was about to make the biggest mistake of my life.

CHAPTER 18

For several moments I watched Dan's face as he struggled to prevent his anger from erupting. I don't know what I dreaded more — that he'd fail, and I'd be crushed by his scathing comments, or that he'd succeed and I'd never know what was really in his mind.

"You're going home," he said at last, managing to hang on to a calm voice that seemed all the more lethal for its lack of emotion. "Just like that."

"No, not just like that, but I —"

"Never mind that Gladys is happily planning a risky expansion because she thinks you'll be there to help her. Never mind that Gillian is banking on you being there to support her business venture. Never mind that there are three little kids out there who think they've found a replacement for the granny they lost."

"Wait a minute —"

"Never mind that you've encouraged people to form attachments, only to turn your back on them when things get a little too serious for comfort."

Okay, so I could see where his pride was hurt, but it wasn't fair of him to bring Gladys and Gillian into the argument. Bristling with resentment, I faced him. "I never made any promises to anyone. I always intended to go back home, and I never pretended otherwise."

"Then why did you stay so long? What's waiting for you back there that's so bloody important you can just walk out on everyone who's relying on you?"

"My home, my job, my friends."

He raised his eyebrows. "And you've got all that sitting there just waiting for you to get back to it, right?"

"Well . . ." No, I didn't. I didn't have a home, or a job. The only real friend I had was Val, and she wasn't exactly counting the minutes until my return. I refused to admit as much to him. "Seattle is my home. America is my home. I can't just leave it and go live in another country."

"Millions of people do. Home is where your heart is, not where your birth certificate is issued."

He didn't understand, and I couldn't tell

him. How could I tell him that as much as I wanted to, I couldn't let myself love him. I just couldn't bear to be second best to anyone ever again.

"You're no different than the rest of us, Marge." He turned away from me and stared out the window at the churning ocean. "We're all looking for something. Anything that will give us a rock to hold on to, a place to belong. It isn't a village or a town or a country, it's people who give us that place."

The ache in my chest was so bad I was afraid I'd cry out. "I think we'd better go."

He turned so swiftly he made me jump. Gripping my arms, he pulled me against him. "Damn it, Marge, why won't you let go for once? I know it's there, but you're so bloody stubborn. . . ."

His mouth came down hard on mine and for a long moment all I could do was kiss him back while the questions raged in my mind. Why couldn't I just trust him to love me? How could I throw away everything this man could give me, when I wanted him so much?

He let me go and stood back. I could see the anger and hurt in his eyes, and I had to fight to hold back the tears. His voice was no longer calm, but shook with emotion when he spoke. "You'll never find what you want, Marge, unless you learn to give all the way. No doubts, no holding back. Just go for it. That's the kind of love that lasts."

The kind he had with his first wife. He didn't say it, but I could almost hear the words in his mind. It confirmed what I already knew. No one would ever take her place. Nor was I about to try. In my misery, I deliberately misunderstood him.

"Well, that might be all right for a horny teenager, but I have more respect for my body than to fall in bed with the first man who asks me."

He looked as if I'd smacked him. "If that's what you think of me, then you're right. It's time you went home."

I let him lead me down that narrow, winding staircase, thinking how fortunate he'd gone first. If he hadn't, I might have thought about throwing myself down the steps.

We didn't speak to each other until he pulled up outside the tea shop. I thanked him for taking me to the lighthouse, and winced when he simply nodded in reply. I dragged myself out of the car, and resisted the urge to watch him drive off.

The bell jangled in my ears as I opened the door and went inside. A couple of women enjoying afternoon tea looked up and waved to me. I managed a weak smile and hurried across the room to the stairs.

Gladys called out to me, but I pretended not to hear. I needed to get to my room before the dam building up behind my eyes burst into a torrent of tears.

Just as I closed the door behind me, my cell phone trilled its serenade. Heart pounding with hope, I flipped it open. Gillian's voice answered, surprising me enough to curb the urgent need to cry.

"I'm sorry to bother you," she said, "but I didn't know who else to ask. You're the only one I know with a car that's home and —"

Knowing it had to be an emergency for her to call me, I interrupted. "It's okay. What's happened?"

"It's the kids. The school bus has broken down and they're stranded out at the school. One of the mothers went out to pick up the kids but she didn't have enough room for mine. I can't get hold of Ned, he's out in the fields and it's starting to rain. . . ."

"Of course I'll get them. I —"

A loud beeping interrupted me and Gillian asked sharply, "What's that?"

"My phone. It needs recharging. Tell me where they are."

I found a pen and scribbled down the directions. "Don't worry," I told her. "I'll find them."

She was still thanking me when the phone died. I plugged it into the charger then rushed down the stairs, just as Gladys came out of the kitchen with a tray loaded with a teapot, china and a double-tiered plate of sandwiches and scones.

"Where are you off to?" she asked, as I followed her into the tearoom. "You just got back."

I garbled an explanation and flew out of the door. Gillian was right. It had started to rain.

Someone had parked a car in front of mine at the garage, and I had to wait for one of the mechanics to move it before I could back out. By the time I found the lane that would take me out to the school, the rain streamed down my windshield too fast for the wipers to clear it.

The kids stood under the porch, all three of them huddled together. Robbie was the first to see me. He ran out and threw himself into my outstretched arms as I leaned out of the car to hug him. Laughing, he scrambled into the car, his sister and brother close behind him.

As I listened to their chatter, the dreadful ache under my ribs began to ease. I was reluctant to take them straight home. They helped keep my mind off my misery, and all I had waiting for me at the tea shop was an empty room and a bleak future.

I threw the suggestion over my shoulder. "How would you guys like to go into town for an ice cream?"

Three yells of excitement answered me. Instead of heading back to the cottage, I turned in the opposite direction and drove toward the town.

Several minutes later we all sat drying out in a cozy booth in the back of Barley's Ice Cream Parlor. All three kids ordered a chocolate sundae, while I settled for a latte. I was in desperate need of comfort, and needed the soothing warmth of coffee.

It occurred to me that I should call Gillian, but my cell phone was back in my room, and the shop was full of customers.

Instead, I told the kids to hurry, and hoped Gillian would know they'd be okay with me.

Still steeped in the bitter memory of the argument with Dan, I paid little attention to what went on around me. The kids chattered among themselves and I listened with part of my mind, while the rest of it wrestled with all the things I should have said or not said. One thing seemed fairly clear. I'd pretty much blown my relationship with Dan.

I tried to tell myself it was for the best. I'd rather be alone for the rest of my life than love a man whose heart belonged to someone else. Been there, done that.

"I am too old enough, aren't I, Nana?"

I dragged myself back to the present, and smiled at Robbie. "Old enough for what, honey?"

"To ride a motorbike. I want a motorbike for my birthday."

Sheila and Craig hooted with laughter. Robbie looked about to cry and I put my arm around him. "Maybe not a motorbike just yet," I whispered in his ear. "But I'm sure we can come up with a surprise just as good."

His little face lit up with excitement. "What surprise?"

"Well, now, if I tell you that, it won't be a surprise, will it?"

He bounced up and down on his seat. "I want to know now."

All three kids stared at me in expectation.

"Not until your birthday," I said firmly. "Now finish your ice cream. It's time to go home."

They all looked disappointed, but did what I asked. I wanted to hug all three of them. I'd have to come up with a really good surprise for all three birthdays, I promised myself.

The rain still pelted down as we left the ice-cream parlor, and I made the kids run to the car. Robbie argued with his brother over whose turn it was to sit in front, and I insisted all three of them sit in the back to settle it.

At last we pulled up outside the cottage and the kids piled out. As Craig opened the gate Gillian came running down the path toward us.

I was expecting her thanks, and was shocked when she yelled at me. "Where have you been? I've been worried sick." She put one arm around Robbie and pulled Sheila against her with the other as if protecting them both.

I started to explain, but when I mentioned the ice cream parlor she yelled again. "Ice cream? You were sitting there enjoying ice cream while I'm sitting here tearing my hair out and wondering if I should ring the police? I thought you'd had an accident. I've been out of my mind with worry."

Sick with guilt, I stammered, "I'm sorry, Gillian. I would have called but I didn't have my phone —"

"You should have brought them straight

home." She gave Sheila a hard shake. "You know better than that. What have I told you about coming straight home from school?"

"It's not her fault —" I began, but Sheila interrupted me.

"Don't shout at Nana!" She stamped her foot. "We was having fun. A lot more fun than you. I hate you." She pulled away from her mother and started up the path. "I don't wanna live with you anymore. I wanna live with Nana, so there."

Once more Gillian launched an attack. "Now look what you've done. Turning my kids against me now. You're good at that, aren't you. You started with my dad and now my kids."

I tried again to protest but she cut me off.

"Why did you have to come here, anyway? They're not your grandkids so you can just stop calling them that. Why don't you go back where you bloody came from."

She stomped off, with a sobbing Robbie beside her and Craig trailing miserably behind.

Stunned, I got back into the car. I could understand Gillian's reaction. I knew how relief could manifest into anger, and I had been incredibly thoughtless. Maybe if I'd had children of my own I'd have been a little more sensitive to a mother's concerns about her kids' well-being. Though I had to admit, that was no excuse.

What upset me most, however, was her accusation. Her words still rang in my head like mallets hammering in nails. *You started with my dad and now my kids.* After all that had been said between us, she still blamed me for Brandon's rejection of her and her mother. It seemed unlikely now that would ever change.

I'd had quite a day. The last place I wanted to be right then was my lonely room, but I figured I'd better lock myself in there before I did any more damage.

Gladys called out from the kitchen when I got back, and when I didn't answer she came to the door. "Gillian's been ringing every fifteen minutes or so. She's looking for her kids."

"They're at home," I said shortly. "Where they belong." I kept climbing and reached the door of my room.

Gladys called up behind me. "Come and join me for a cuppa."

I wasn't in the mood for tea and crumpets. "I'm tired, Gladys. I'll be down later, okay?" Before she could argue I shut the door.

The next hour or so passed in a blur of pain and self-loathing. I'd destroyed the two relationships that had meant the most to me. I'd been offered the chance to have what I'd always dreamed of having — a real family. Not to mention someone I could love the way a woman should love a man.

I wondered what Val would say when I told her what I'd done. I could just hear her, telling me what a fool I was, what a miserable coward.

Oh, Dan. I doubled over, hugging my aching body. I missed him already. Even more than I'd missed Brandon. Unlike my late husband, I knew I'd go on missing Dan until the day I died.

Well, Val, you were right. Without risking, there's no living.

If only I'd been strong enough to take the risk. Maybe second best would have been better than not at all. Now I'd never know.

I spent the next few days either in my room or walking along the cliffs. I avoided Gladys as much as possible. I kept up the accounts but stayed away from e-mail. I wasn't ready to admit to Val what an idiot I'd been.

A dozen times a day I picked up my phone, but my stupid pride wouldn't let me call Dan, or Gillian. I knew I would have to deal with Gillian sooner or later, but I kept putting it off. As for Dan, I figured if he'd really wanted to see me again, he would have come by. As it was, he stayed away from the tearoom, much to Gladys's dismay.

Finally, one wet afternoon, I came home from a long walk and decided I should answer Val's e-mails, or I'd be losing her, too. As usual Gladys called my name as I passed the kitchen door, and as usual, I pretended not to hear her.

Val's e-mails were full of complaints about her bookkeeper, and again asked me when I was coming home. I stared at the words on the screen for a long time, then I signed off without answering her. Instead, I went into the kitchen, where Gladys sat reading the local newspaper.

She looked up as I walked in, her face alight with pleasant surprise. "I was just coming up to your room," she said. "I've got something to give you."

I hated to disappoint her, but I'd made up my mind. "I've come to a decision," I said. "It's time I went back to the States. I'm booking a flight for a week from today."

Her mouth tightened and she dropped her gaze. "Is this because of you and Dan or you and Gillian?"

I swallowed past the lump in my throat and sat down at the table. "Both, I guess. I didn't expect anything from Dan, but I hoped that in time Gillian would stop hat-ing me for ruining her life. I guess that's not going to happen. If only we knew what really happened between Brandon and Eileen, we might have been able to come to some kind of understanding."

"So now you're just going to run away from it all."

Resentment stirred, and I took a deep breath. "I came here hoping for answers, Gladys. All I've got is more heartache. I think it would be better for everyone if I went home."

Gladys folded the newspaper with slow, deliberate movements that told me she was turning something over in her mind. Then she laid the paper down and looked at me over her glasses. "Pour yourself a cup of tea, dearie," she said. "It's time you knew the whole story.

"Eileen confided in me," Gladys said, while I sat there staring at her in shock. "She made me promise not to tell Gillian."

I struggled to understand. "You've known all this time? Why didn't you tell me before?"

Gladys leaned her elbows on the table. "I wanted to. I didn't think it was my place. Eileen trusted me to keep it a secret. I couldn't tell it to a stranger."

"And now?"

She shrugged. "I think Eileen would want me to tell her story now. I promised not to tell Gillian. I didn't promise not to tell you. It will be up to you to decide if she should hear it."

"I'm not sure I want to hear the story." I'd taken too long reaching my decision to go home. I was afraid this would only complicate things and further prevent me from leaving. I couldn't be sure that it would make a difference in Gillian's opinion of me. More to the point, I didn't want to be in Miles End without Dan.

"You and Gillian need each other." Gladys crossed her arms. "Maybe it will help if you both know the truth."

"All right. I'll listen. But that doesn't mean I'll tell Gillian. It might be better to leave things the way they are. Eileen obviously thought so."

"Listen to what I have to say, then you decide." She hoisted herself off her chair. "Let's get comfortable."

I followed her into the living room, my heart pounding with apprehension. Something told me that what I was about to hear would alter the future for all of us.

CHAPTER 19

I sat in the armchair and waited for Gladys to get settled. She seemed to take forever, but finally she leaned back with a contented sigh. "It'll be so good to get this off my chest."

Good for whom, I wondered, but then she started talking.

"Eileen met Brandon when he went to Chatswell on business. Eileen was barmaid in a pub there."

Just like my mother, I thought, stunned by the coincidence.

"Brandon took Eileen out every night for two weeks," Gladys said. "When he went back, he wrote to her. They wrote back and forth for about two years, with him flying in to see her as often as he could. Then she found out she was having Gillian."

I flinched. That was still a sore point with me. "That must have been a shock for him," I said drily.

"Well, she wrote and told him, and he came back here to ask her to marry him. Told her he wanted her to live in America." Gladys shook her head. "She told him she couldn't. Too scared she was, to leave her home. Brandon didn't like that at all. Said that if she loved him she'd go with him."

"Maybe he was right." The parallel was close enough to make me uncomfortable. Would I have stayed if Dan had loved me enough? Could I have loved him enough to turn my back on all that I'd known and everything I'd been to start over in a new and, in many ways, an alien world?

One thing I did know. Those questions would haunt me the rest of my life.

"You have to know Eileen to understand," Gladys said. "She wasn't exactly what you'd call adventurous. Most people here wouldn't move away from the village they grew up in, leave alone go to a foreign country. That's the way we are. America seemed like a scary place in the seventies. Riots going on. Famous people getting killed. Everybody on drugs. I wouldn't have wanted to go there."

"Not all of us were spaced-out flower children," I murmured.

She looked uncomfortable. "Well, you know what I mean. It was a long road from this quiet little village. That's all I'm saying."

"If Brandon really loved Eileen, why didn't he stay here?"

"He told her he couldn't make a living here. Not like he could in America. He said he wanted a good life for her and the baby and he couldn't give her that here."

"He was probably right about that."

"Well, if you ask me, he was selfish. Most men are. He wanted things his way or not at all. He kept arguing and arguing with Eileen until she didn't know which way to turn."

I could imagine how hard he pressured her. Brandon never did like opposition when he wanted something.

"She finally got so upset she told him she didn't love him enough to go with him. Not only that, she said she hated him for getting her in trouble. Her parents had thrown her out of the house when they found out about the baby, and she was living in a rotten little flat all by herself. She told Brandon he'd ruined her life, and she didn't want her baby to have a father like him. She said she never wanted to see him again."

Poor Brandon. Now I began to understand that sadness in his eyes. "So he went back home without her," I said, more to myself than to Gladys.

"Yes, he did. Before he went, though, he told her he'd make sure no woman ever did that to him again. Three months later he wrote and told her he'd had an operation so he couldn't have kids. If he couldn't have hers, he didn't want none at all."

Dear God. No wonder he'd never been able to love me. How deeply hurt he must have been to do something that drastic.

We must have met soon after that. I was alone and needy. Still hurting from that rejection, he'd married me on the rebound. No matter how much he might have regretted that later, I knew Brandon had far too much pride to admit he'd made a mistake. Even to himself.

Shaken by what I'd learned, I had to force my concentration back to Gladys.

"A little while after that," Gladys said, "Eileen wrote to him. Told him she'd changed her mind. Said she'd go to America, as long as they could get married in England. She got a letter back from him right away. He told her it was too late. He was married, and he wasn't going to leave his wife. He bought her the cottage, but he never went back to see her or Gillian."

Tears I didn't know were there suddenly spilled out and rolled down my cheeks. I'd cried for myself before, but now I cried for them — Brandon, Eileen and Gillian. What a sad, tragic story.

Gladys struggled to her feet, walked over to the desk and plucked a box of tissues from inside the flap. "Eileen never told Gillian that she was the one who'd sent Brandon away," she said, as she handed me the box. "She was afraid Gillian would never forgive her for what she'd done. So she told her that her father had met someone else and married her instead."

Gladys sat down and held out her hands in front of the gas fire to warm them. "I suppose Brandon was too heartbroken to try and see his little daughter. Would have upset him too much. It was easier for him just to pretend she didn't exist."

I blew my nose. "No, it was his pride. He'd messed up their lives and he didn't want anyone to know about it. If only he'd told me about Eileen and the baby, we might have been able to work things out."

Would it have been better for me to know the truth and let him go, knowing he didn't love me, rather than spend all those empty years without the love and affection I'd craved? Maybe. One thing I did know in my heart — that Brandon left me the cottage as his way of putting things right. He wanted me to know what he'd had too much pride to tell me. He wanted me to know his daughter.

"So now it's up to you," Gladys said, disturbing my thoughts. "Whatever you tell Gillian, I'm glad I told you."

"I am, too." I smiled at her, then glanced at the clock. "I'm going over to see her. Right now."

"I'm glad." She got up and put her arms around me in a bear hug. "Maybe now you'll think twice about staying."

I pulled back from her. "I don't know about that. I don't know how Gillian will feel about things, even if she does know the truth. But I think she deserves to hear it."

"So do I." Gladys went back to the desk and opened it. "I almost forgot to give you this." She handed me a white envelope. My name was scribbled on the front of it, but nothing else.

"It's from Dan, dearie. He stopped by to see you, but he had things to do and couldn't wait until you got back." Gladys patted my shoulder. "I think you'd better read it right away."

I wanted to tear it open right then and there, but I curbed my impatience. "I'll take it upstairs," I said awkwardly. "I left my phone up there and I need to call Gillian before I go over there."

Gladys nodded and I rushed up the stairs, stumbling in my haste to get to my room. I sank on the bed, then stared at the envelope, afraid to open it for fear it wouldn't say what I wanted it to say. When I did start to read, I felt a chill like nothing I'd ever experienced before.

I couldn't let you go without saying goodbye. I've got a job in Chatswell, and I'm leaving in the morning. If you have time to stop by this evening, I'll be home.
Yours, Dan.

I felt as if the sun had gone out, leaving a bleak world behind. Yes, I know I'd decided to go home. But that was my decision, to change if I wanted.

I stared at the scrawled lines again. *I couldn't let you go without saying goodbye.* It sounded so final. I didn't know if I could do that. I didn't know if I could see him again, knowing it was for the last time.

My hand felt lifeless as I flipped open the phone and punched Gillian's number. The line was busy. I waited in numb misery for five minutes and tried again. The line was still busy. I couldn't sit in that room any longer. I'd drive over there, I decided, and take a chance she was home. I'd make her listen to me.

I went back down to tell Gladys I was leaving.

"I know what's in the letter, dearie," she said, as I turned to go. "Dan told me he wanted to say goodbye."

I nodded, too miserable to look at her. "I don't know how I'm going to say goodbye to him."

"He wants to see you. He doesn't want to say goodbye, either."

Struggling against the false hope, I mumbled, "Did he say that?"

"He didn't have to. I know Dan. He wants you to tell him not to go. He's leaving the choice up to you." She came up behind me. "I'll tell you this much, dearie. If you don't go to see him tonight, you'll probably never see him again. He has his pride, you know."

Pride. It had ruined so many lives already. Even I had been too proud to call Dan. Or Gillian. Well, it was time I let go of the doubts and go for it. Dan was right. "I'll go see him. After I've talked to Gillian."

Gladys nodded, and I swear I saw tears in her eyes. "That's my good girl," she said softly.

It was dark by the time I got to the cottage. A light burned in the window, so I knew someone was home. Sheila answered the door, her face lighting up when she saw me. She shouted over her shoulder, "Nana's here! Nana's here!"

Craig appeared behind her, looking worried. "Mum's upstairs with Robbie. He's ill."

I hesitated. "Do you think she'd mind if I came in?"

"Course not." He pushed Sheila out of the way. "Come in."

Sheila shoved him back, then hugged my waist. "Where have you been? We missed you. Mummy tried to ring you but she couldn't get an answer."

My pulse quickened. "She tried to call? When?"

"A little while ago. She's been calling everybody. Robbie's really ill."

"Where is your mom?" I headed for the stairs as I asked the question.

Craig answered me. "In our bedroom. Here, I'll show you." He raced up the stairs with me hot on his heels and Sheila dragging after me.

All my worries about how to approach Gillian vanished when I saw her. She was kneeling by the bed, one hand lying on Robbie's chest. I could hear the rattle from where I stood in the doorway.

She looked at me, and the fear in her eyes jumped out at me. "He's burning hot. I rang the doctor. He's at the hospital. The nurse told me to take Robbie there, but I can't find Ned." She turned back to her child. "Look at him. He can't breathe."

I hurried over to the bed and laid my hand on Robbie's forehead. It was like touching a heating pad turned on high. "Get him wrapped up in a blanket," I said. "We'll take him to the hospital."

Gillian looked frightened. "What about the kids? Ned should be home by now. I don't know where he is."

"We'll drop them off at The Tea Parlor." I turned to Craig. "Find me some paper and a pen to write a note."

He fled down the stairs and I followed him. It took him only a moment to find pen and paper, and I jotted down a note to Ned, telling him where we were going and to pick up the kids at the tea shop.

I got Craig and Sheila bundled into their coats and by that time Gillian appeared on the stairs, carrying Robbie in her arms. Her face looked white and drawn, and her terror seemed to fill the room.

"He'll be fine," I told her. "They'll know what to do at the hospital."

"I should have rung for an ambulance,"

she said, as I headed down the road with her and Robbie seated next to me and the other two in the back. "But I thought by the time it came all the way out here and back again, it would be quicker if I took him. I kept thinking Ned would be home any minute. I rang the farmhouse. They said he left half an hour ago. Where can he be? He's never home after dark."

She peered anxiously at the road ahead as if she expected him to be there any minute.

"He's probably held up somewhere," I told her. "Try not to worry. He'll find the note and Gladys can tell him what's happening."

"I rang you, too." Gillian rocked back and forth, clutching Robbie close to her body. "But there was no answer."

"I left my phone upstairs while I talked to Gladys. I'm so sorry."

"Well, then I called for a taxi, but he was on his way to Chatswell."

Robbie started to cry — a weak, wailing sound that sent shivers down my back.

Gillian held him closer. "It's all right, lovey. Mummy's taking you to a nice place where they'll make you feel better."

"Is Robbie going to die?" Sheila asked, her voice high with fear.

"No, he's going to be just fine," I assured

her, wishing I felt as confident as I sounded. Robbie's breathing had become more labored, and now he no longer cried. He just lay there in Gillian's arms with his eyes closed, his little chest heaving with his effort to force air into his lungs.

I gripped the wheel, and prayed as I'd never prayed before.

We left the kids with Gladys and a few minutes later we headed up the road to Stattenham. It seemed to me an awful long way to have to go for emergency care. I was used to a city that had a clinic within easy reach no matter where you lived.

It didn't help matters that the road curved and twisted on its way to town, and had no streetlamps. I'd only driven it once at night, and then I'd had Dan showing me the way.

Dan. In all the upheaval, I'd forgotten about him. He was waiting for me. Waiting to say goodbye.

Maybe I'd have time, I thought, when Robbie was safely settled in the hands of the doctors. If not, I'd have to call Dan and hope he would understand.

I put him out of my mind then, and concentrated on getting to town as fast and as safely as possible. By the time we arrived at the emergency ward, Robbie was unconscious.

The next few minutes passed in a blur of activity as nurses and orderlies hustled the little boy onto a gurney and raced down the long hallway.

Tears ran down Gillian's face as she pleaded with them to let her go with her son, but a stout nurse with an imposing voice ordered us into the waiting room.

An elderly man and woman sat close together in one corner, earnestly whispering to each other. After making Gillian sit down in a deep armchair on the other side of the room, I found a coffee machine and filled two cups. I gave one to her, and then grasped her free hand. "He's going to be all right," I told her. "I know it."

Her eyes looked huge in her white face. She'd dragged her hair back and fastened it behind her ears with a metal hair clip, and the baggy blue sweater she wore gaped at the neck. She looked older, tired, utterly beaten, and my heart went out to her.

I put my coffee down, took the cup out of her hand and put that down, too. Then I wrapped my arms around her and held her while she sobbed.

It was only a minute or two, but it felt much longer that we sat there together, both of us in tears. Finally she recovered some control, and pulled away from me. Hunting for a tissue in her pocket, she said unsteadily, "Thank you. I don't know what I would have done without you."

I was about to answer when I heard the jingle on my cell phone. Ned's voice almost shouted in my ear. I handed the phone to Gillian and anxiously watched her face as she talked to her husband.

She fought to hold back tears as she explained everything that had happened. Then she listened for a while. "No," she said, after a few moments. "I don't want the children here. It will only frighten them. I'll be home as soon as I can. I'll ring you if there's any news."

She paused, then a tear slid down her cheek as she whispered, "Me, too."

"He's going to take care of the kids," she said, as she handed me back the phone. "He had a flat tire. That's why he was late getting home."

She looked as if she wanted to say something else, so I waited.

After chewing on her lip for a moment, she added, "I'm sorry about the other day."

"It was my fault," I said quickly. "I should have brought the children straight home. I'm so sorry."

She shook her head. "You were just giving them a treat. I shouldn't have been that cross. Only I was scared something bad had happened to my kids. If anything happened to any of them . . ." Again tears prevented her from finishing.

I waited for her to mop up her face and then handed her the coffee. "Here, drink this. It might help."

She emptied the cup and put it back on the table. "You know something? That was the first time in years that Ned told me he loved me."

Her smile was beautiful to see.

"I'm glad he said it tonight," I said, my throat so tight I could hardly get the words out.

"Me, too. I —" The light drained from her face again and she shot to her feet. Looking up, I saw a man in a white coat hurrying toward us, and once more I prayed.

"Mrs. Hodge?" He was dark-skinned, with bright, intelligent eyes, a strong accent and an unpronounceable name. "Your little boy is resting comfortably right now. It looks as if he might have a touch of pneumonia, but we have him in a tent and we're pumping antibiotics in him. We'll know better by the morning, but I'd say he's going to be all right."

Gillian looked as if she wanted to hug him. "Can I see him?"

"Just for a minute. He's sleeping right now but you can take a peek. Then we have to let him rest."

Gillian glanced at me. "Can she come, too?"

The doctor gave me a quick inspection. "Only family right now. I'm sorry."

"Marjorie is family," Gillian said. "She's my stepmother."

She was much too concerned about Robbie to realize that the tears running down my cheeks were for the words she'd just spoken. Once more, a single sentence had the power to change my life.

One day I'd tell her what those words had meant to me. One day I'd tell her that in that simple sentence she'd given me a gift more precious than she could possibly imagine. One day, when we could sit down and look upon this time as the beginning of a long and beautiful friendship. I hoped, with all my heart, that one day wasn't too far away.

CHAPTER 20

As we followed the doctor down the brightly lit corridor to Robbie's room, my elation faded. I dreaded seeing that little boy so sick and helpless.

A strong smell of disinfectant greeted us when we went in. Machines blinked and hummed behind the plastic curtain, and Robbie looked so tiny — so utterly lonely.

I ached to hold him. I could only imagine how Gillian must have felt, being so close to her sick child and forbidden to touch him. I reached for her hand and squeezed.

Without looking at me, she returned the pressure. Neither of us had said a word, but in that first physical contact we'd shared a moment I knew neither of us would ever forget.

The doctor ushered us out after a minute or two, and we walked side by side back to the waiting room.

"You don't have to wait," Gillian said. "I'll

be all right now if you want to go home."

It was then that I remembered Dan again. "Would you like me to go back to the cottage so that Ned can be with you?" I glanced at my watch. Maybe I could call Dan and have him meet me at Gillian's.

"No, I don't think so. Gladys fed the kids and he'll have them in bed soon. They've got school tomorrow, and they need their sleep."

"Well, you'd better call him anyway." I gave her the phone. "He'll be waiting to hear."

She took it from me, and for the next few minutes she talked to Ned and the kids while I sat struggling with indecision.

I kept hearing Gladys's voice. *If you don't go to see him tonight, you'll probably never see him again.*

I jumped when Gillian handed me my phone. "Thanks," she said, and I was relieved to see some color creep into her cheeks. "They'll be okay. Now you just go on home."

"I'm not leaving you alone here. I do have to make a quick phone call, all right?"

She nodded and picked up a magazine. "Take your time."

I hurried away from her and made for the entrance. This was a call I needed to make in private. I reached my car in the parking garage, unlocked it and climbed in.

Shivering more from apprehension than the cold, damp air outside, I punched in Dan's number. I waited for his line to ring, wishing I'd rehearsed what to say. All I hoped was that he'd be willing to listen. The rest would have to come from my heart.

The line rang and rang. I counted ten of them before I finally hung up. Of course. If he was moving out tomorrow, his phone had more than likely been shut off.

I thought of asking Gladys to go down there and tell him what had happened, but dismissed it a second later. Gladys didn't drive. She'd have to call for the cab and that was probably somewhere between Miles End and Chatswell.

I sat there in the shadows of that cold, lonely parking garage and let the misery seep into me. Maybe this was God's way of telling me Dan and I weren't meant to be.

When I felt I had control of my emotions again, I climbed out of the car and hurried back to Gillian. She sat where I'd left her. The couple had gone, leaving us alone.

"It looks as if this will be a long night," I said, as Gillian laid down the magazine. "So we have plenty of time."

She looked wary. "Time for what?"

I smiled. "Time for you to hear the story I have to tell you."

I told her then, every word that Gladys had told me. I didn't stop there. She listened without comment, various expressions flashing across her face as I talked about my childhood, my marriage, Brandon's lack of emotion and my longing for the affection I never knew.

I wondered if she was making comparisons to her own life, and maybe saw herself in the mirror of mine.

She was quiet for a moment when I reached the end of my lengthy account. Then she said quietly, "He wanted us to meet, didn't he. That's why he left you the cottage."

"That's what I believe."

She looked at me, weariness etched in her face. "I'm glad."

I smiled. "Me, too."

"It's terrible what pride can do."

"Yes," I said. "It is indeed." The look we exchanged said it all. It would take time, and we wouldn't always see eye to eye, but we were family. We'd make it work.

Later that night we dozed in the comfortable armchairs, and woke up to the news that Robbie's fever had broken. All being well, he would be going home in a couple of days. As we hugged each other, everything seemed perfectly clear. At last I knew what I wanted to do.

"I've made a decision," I told Gladys a few days later. We sat in the living room warming our toes in front of the fire. Business had been slow all day, and we'd closed the shop early.

Gladys looked up from the papers she'd been studying. "Funny you should say that. I've made one, too."

"Really? What is it?"

"You first."

"All right." I took a deep breath. After all, it was one of the most important decisions in my life. Once I'd announced my intentions, there'd be no going back. "I've decided to stay here in England. I'm not going back to the States."

Gladys's reaction was disappointing. "That's nice."

"You don't sound very surprised."

"I'm not."

I sighed. "Does everyone know me better than I know myself?"

"No, dearie. Just a few of us."

I gave her a sharp look, but she refused to meet my gaze. "So what is your decision?" I asked. "I hope it's more exciting than mine."

For an answer, she handed me the sheaf of papers.

"What's this?" I scanned the top page. Thinking I'd misunderstood, I read it again. I looked up to find her beaming at me. "This says . . ."

"I'm making you a full partner in the tea shop. All you have to do is sign it. That's if you want it, of course."

I gaped at her. "Want it? Of course I want it, but I don't understand, I —"

"Look, you do all the book work, you know all about running a business. Much more than I do. If I'm going to expand the way we talked about, I'll need someone with a good head on their shoulders to help me. I can't think of anyone I'd want more than you."

"But I don't know if I can afford to buy in —"

"You don't need to. We'll get a business loan, like you said, and we'll muddle along until the tea shop is paying for itself. It might be a little dodgy at first, but I'm sure we can make a go of it. When I'm gone, it will be all yours. What do you say?"

I got up and threw my arms around her. "It's an incredible, generous offer," I said, "and I accept. We'll make it a success, you'll see." I sat down again and stretched out my legs. "How did you know I'd stay?"

"Gillian told me you talked in the hospital. I hoped you'd stay after that, but just to make sure, I had my lawyer draw up the papers. I thought that between Gillian and me, we could persuade you not to go back to America." She lowered her chin until she could see over her glasses. "I must say, it was a lot easier than we thought."

"It wasn't an easy decision to make." I remembered the agony of the past few days, and how I'd fought against the temptation to run away from it all and go home. Dan had left town without trying to contact me, and had left no phone number or address. Miles End without him was a miserable prospect.

Then again, I'd argued with myself, if I stayed, there was always a slim chance that I'd bump into him again. It was that slim hope that had tipped the scales.

"I know it wasn't easy," Gladys said. "But it was the right decision. You'll see."

Two days later I thought about that remark. I was in the tearoom with Lesley, the new girl, showing her how to set the tables. The doorbell jangled, and I looked up to see Dan weaving his way toward me.

I froze, and the forks fell from my hand with a clatter onto the table. I could feel

Lesley staring at me, but I couldn't seem to make my tongue work.

Dan smiled at her first, then looked at me. "Hello, Marge."

I nodded, painfully aware of Lesley's eager ears as she pretended to be absorbed in turning cups upside down in their saucers.

"Gladys told me about the partnership," Dan said. "Congratulations."

"Thank you." Now that he was here, I wished he hadn't come back. *Why had he come back?* All I could think about was what Lesley must think of these two middle-aged people acting like awkward teenagers.

"Er . . . I suppose that means you won't be going back to Seattle."

"No . . . I mean, yes . . . no." I wished to hell he'd leave. All the longing I'd tried to ignore came rushing back. God, I wanted this man. In every possible meaning of the word.

I'd never been that excited about sex with Brandon. Most of the time it had been something to get through — the price I paid for the security that had once been so important to me.

Now all I could think about was lying naked in bed with Dan Connelly. I felt like that horny teenager I'd scorned in the lighthouse, embracing the erotic fantasies

I'd forbidden my mind to explore over the past few months.

I wanted him all over me, but that stupid remark I'd spit at him that last day would ensure that never happened. I couldn't think of a way to take those words back.

That hurt, uncertain look I hated appeared on his face. "Well, I'd better get along here. I just wanted to stop and congratulate you."

My face ached with the effort to hold my smile. "Thanks. How's the new job going?"

"It's okay. I miss working for myself, though." For a moment he looked deep into my eyes. "I miss a lot of things."

The next second he was heading for the door and out of my life.

The bell jangled mournfully behind him as he disappeared.

"That was weird," Lesley said, while I just stood there, staring at the spot where he'd been.

"What was?"

I didn't really want an answer, but I got one anyway.

"He looked, well, you know, sort of lost. Like he didn't really know what he was saying. Probably been drinking, that's what." She shook her head and went back to arranging the china.

Lost. That's what I'd be without him. Maybe he'd never love me the way he'd loved his first wife, but that didn't mean he couldn't love me in a different way.

"I've got to leave," I told Lesley. "Just finish the tables then ask Gladys what she needs you to do." I didn't wait for her answer. I was out of the door before I gave myself time to think.

I saw Dan's car pulling away from the curb and I started running after him. I yelled his name, over and over, not even caring that several women in the street paused to stare at me.

Terrified I'd left it too late, I rushed out into the middle of the road, hoping he'd see me in his rearview mirror. Just then a boy ran across in front of him, and he had to brake.

It gave me enough time to reach his car and I pounded on the window. I felt weak with relief when he rolled it down and stared at me, his face stiff with shock.

"What the hell are you doing?"

"Chasing after you, of course." I opened the door. "Get out."

"I'm in the middle of the road."

"I know. Just get out."

He stared at me for another second or two, then eased out of the car.

I stepped up close to him and looked into his eyes. "If I booked a room at the inn for tonight, would you spend the night with me?"

He'd never know the effort it had cost me to say those words, but his answer was worth all the fear of making a fool of myself. He didn't speak, just folded his arms around me and kissed me the way we'd kissed that beautiful Christmas afternoon.

It all came together for me right then. There was so much promise in that kiss, so much warmth and excitement. Like heated honey, it seeped into my mind and heart, filling up all the empty spaces etched by bitterness and pain. My future held more than I'd ever dreamed, and now the past and all its hurt faded into the mists of time. I had everything a woman could want — a family, a satisfying career and the blessing of love. Now I had it all.

"You do know that half the town is watching us," Dan said, when he finally let me go.

"Yes," I told him. "And you know what? I don't care."

"Good." He caught my hand and led me around to the passenger side of the car. "They'd better get used to it. They'll be seeing a lot of it from now on." He dropped another kiss on my forehead. "Welcome home."

Home. Such a great word. It conjured up visions of families gathered around a dinner table, warm nights by the fire, schooldays and holidays, and growing old together.

Yes, at last I was truly home.

ABOUT THE AUTHOR

Doreen Roberts lives with her husband, who is also her manager and her biggest fan, in the beautiful city of Portland, Oregon. She believes that everyone should have a little adventure now and again to add interest to their lives. She believes in taking risks and has been known to embark on an adventure or two of her own. She is happiest, however, when she is creating stories about the biggest adventure of all — falling in love and learning to live happily ever after.

The employees of Thorndike Press hope you have enjoyed this Large Print book. All our Thorndike and Wheeler Large Print titles are designed for easy reading, and all our books are made to last. Other Thorndike Press Large Print books are available at your library, through selected bookstores, or directly from us.

For information about titles, please call:

(800) 223-1244

or visit our Web site at:

www.gale.com/thorndike
www.gale.com/wheeler

To share your comments, please write:

Publisher
Thorndike Press
295 Kennedy Memorial Drive
Waterville, ME 04901